THE RANCHER
AND THE BABY

BY
MARIE FERRARELLA

D1393505

MILLS & BOON

First Published in Great Britain 2016
By Mills & Boon, an imprint of HarperCollins*Publishers*
1 London Bridge Street, London, SE1 9GF

© 2016 Marie Rydzynski-Ferrarella

ISBN: 978-0-263-92046-8

23-1216

Our policy is to use papers that are natural, renewable and recyclable products and made from wood grown in sustainable forests. The logging and manufacturing processes conform to the legal environmental regulations of the country of origin.

Printed and bound in Spain
by CPI, Barcelona

Marie Ferrarella is a *USA TODAY* bestselling and RITA®
Award–winning author who has written more than two
hundred and fifty books for Mills & Boon, some under the
name Marie Nicole. Her romances are beloved by fans
worldwide. Visit her website, www.marieferrarella.com.

To
Michael & Mark,
who were once my
younger brothers,
but through the
miracle of creative math,
are now my
older brothers

Prologue

"Mind if I cut in?"

Instantly pulled out of her mental wanderings—a defense mechanism she employed when whoever she was with was boring her out of her mind—Cassidy McCullough looked up, focusing on the man who had just tapped her dance partner's shoulder.

Not that she really needed to.

Despite the fact that he had been absent from Forever for the better part of four years, she would have recognized that voice anywhere.

It popped up in her nightmares.

Will Laredo.

Will had been her brothers' friend for as far back as she could remember—until his estrangement with his father had taken him to parts unknown, simultaneously bringing peace to her own corner of the world.

As she looked back, it felt as if her peace had been far too short-lived. Especially since, for reasons that were beyond her understanding, all three of her brothers liked this six-foot-one-inch, dirty-blond-haired irritant on two legs—which was why Cody had not only invited him to his wedding, he'd made Will one of his groomsmen.

To her surprise, Ron Jenkins, her fawning partner on the dance floor, seemed all too ready to acquiesce to Laredo's casual query. Under normal circumstances, she would have celebrated getting a different partner— but not this time.

Ron might be willing, Cassidy thought, but she damn well wasn't.

"He might not mind," Cassidy retorted defiantly, "but I do."

Rather than taking his cue and backing away, Will remained exactly where he was. Not only that, but his mouth curved in that annoying, smug way of his that she had always hated.

"Your brothers seemed to think I should dance with you."

"Maybe you should dance with one of them since they all seem to be so keen on the subject of dancing," Cassidy informed him.

Looking increasingly more uncomfortable, Ron seemed ready to fade into the shadows. "No, really, it's all right," he assured both her and Will nervously. A slight man, he appeared more than ready to surren-der his claim to her.

Cassidy's eyes narrowed as she froze her partner in place. "You stop dancing with me, Ron Jenkins," she warned the man, "and it'll be the last thing you'll ever remember doing."

Rather than slow down, Cassidy sped up her tempo. Instead of being annoyed or embarrassed at this obvious rejection, Will laughed. "You'd better do as she says, Ron. Most men around here would sooner cross an angry rattlesnake than Cassidy. I hear that her bite is a lot more deadly."

Struggling to hold on to her temper, Cassidy tossed her head. Several blond strands came loose and cascaded to her shoulders. She ignored them.

"If I were you, Laredo, I'd keep that in mind the next time you think about cutting in," she informed him, her eyes blazing.

Will inclined his head, the same amused smile slowly curving his lips. "There's not going to be a next time," he assured her.

Cassidy turned her face up to her partner's and said in a voice intentionally loud enough for Will to overhear, "Dance me by the champagne table, Ron. Now I've got something else to celebrate besides my brother Cody's wedding."

"I would," Ron told her dryly, "if you'd let me lead for a change."

Cassidy could have sworn she heard Will laughing in the background.

She wasn't going to cause a scene, she promised herself. Not here. This was the first wedding in the family, and it was Cody's day. But the moment it was over, she was going to find out which of her three brothers had put Will Laredo up to this, and they were going to pay dearly for it. They knew how she felt about him.

She'd been incensed when she found out that Cody had gotten in contact with Will and asked if he would come and be in his wedding party. When he'd told her about it, she'd almost withdrawn herself, but Connor had talked her out of it, appealing to her sense of family.

"Cassidy," Ron said, raising his voice.

She realized by the look on the man's face that this was not the first time that Ron had tried to get her attention.

"What?" she snapped, then cleared her throat and repeated the word in a more subdued tone—silently damning Laredo. The man had the ability of messing with her mind and ruining any moment just by his being there. "What? Am I leading again?"

"I don't care about that," Ron said, which told her that she was guilty of doing just that. Again.

"Then what?" she asked.

"You're crushing my hand." He looked positively pained.

Embarrassed, as well as annoyed, Cassidy released Jenkins's hand. A more accurate description would have been that she threw it aside and out of her grasp.

To the casual observer from across the floor, had Ron's hand been detached, it would have most likely bounced on the floor and gotten wedged somewhere.

"Man up," she ordered Ron through gritted teeth and then walked away from him just as the band began to play another song.

Out of the corner of her eye, she saw Laredo shaking his head. He made no effort to hide the fact that he was observing her. She felt herself growing angry. Had they not been at her brother's wedding, she would have marched right up to him and demanded to know just what he thought he was shaking his head at.

But they *were* at Cody's wedding, so she couldn't cause a scene, couldn't hold Will accountable or wipe that smug look off his pretty-boy face. It wouldn't look right for the maid of honor to deck one of the grooms-men at her own brother's wedding.

That didn't change the fact that she really wanted to.

Cassidy squared her shoulders and went to get a glass of punch.

Hang in there, she told herself. Come tomorrow, Will Laredo was leaving Forever, going back to wherever it was that he disappeared to when he'd initially left. And then life would go back to being bearable again.

Twelve more hours, she thought. Just twelve more hours.

It felt like an eternity.

Chapter One

Noise had never been a distraction for Olivia Blayne Santiago. She had learned how to effectively tune it out long before her law school days.

Rain, however, was another matter.

While noise, from whatever source, had always been an ongoing part of her day-to-day life and as such could be filed away in the recesses of her mind and matched later to an entire catalog of different sounds, rain demanded immediate attention.

Because rain in this part of Texas could sometimes come under the heading of being a life-or-death matter.

As the first lawyer to open a practice in Forever, Texas—a practice she now ran jointly with Cash Taylor with an eye out for further expansion—Olivia put in rather long hours. This despite the fact that she was married to the town sheriff and had a young, growing family. Between them, she and Cash handled all the legal concerns for the residents of Forever, be those concerns large or small. For the most part, Olivia could do that in her sleep.

But rain was something that always made Olivia

pause, especially when it seemed to give no indication of stopping. What that meant was that a downpour could turn into a flash flood—often without any warning.

Olivia had learned to be leery of the sound of rain on her roof. It had been raining since early morning and gave no sign of stopping.

"This storm looks like it's going to be a bad one," she commented, looking at Cassidy.

Cassidy McCullough had been interning at the law firm for close to four months now, and she saw a great deal of herself in the young woman. Granted she was the firstborn in her family while Cassidy was the last, but Cassidy possessed a spark, a drive to become someone. She wasn't one to just allow herself to float along through life, enjoying each day but never having any sort of an ultimate game plan other than making it through to the end of another week. A go-getter, Cassidy was working for her as an intern even as she was taking online courses at night to complete her postgraduate degree.

They had instantly hit it off, and Olivia had taken an interest in Cassidy from the first day she had walked into the law office.

Since Cassidy hadn't said anything in response to her comment, Olivia raised her voice to get the young woman's attention. "Why don't you call it a day and go home?" she suggested.

Stationed at a small desk in the corner of Olivia's office—a desk that was piled high with stacks of paper—Cassidy glanced up from the report she'd been compiling since she'd come in that morning.

Her brow furrowed slightly as she replayed Olivia's words in her head.

"I can't leave now. I'm not anywhere near finished with this." It wasn't something she would have normally advertised since she took pride in being fast as well as thorough, but if Olivia was considering sending her home, it was something the lawyer needed to know.

Olivia listened again to the rain as it hit the windows. Was it her imagination, or had the rain gotten even more pronounced in the last five minutes? If it got any worse, she wondered if the windows could withstand it.

"If you don't leave now," Olivia warned her, "you may have to sleep on that desk, and I promise that you won't find it very comfortable."

"Why?" Cassidy asked, puzzled. "I mean, I can see why the desk wouldn't be comfortable, but why would I have to sleep on it if I went on working?" She glanced at her watch. "It's not late."

"It's later than you think," Olivia responded, then looked at the younger woman seriously. "Don't you hear that?"

"Hear what?" Cassidy asked uncertainly, scanning the room.

"That." Olivia pointed toward the window when she saw she wasn't getting through to her intern. "The rain," she added for good measure just in case she wasn't making herself clear.

Enlightened, Cassidy nodded. "Oh, that. Of course I hear the rain," she acknowledged. As far as she was concerned, a storm was no big deal. There was always going to be another one. "It was raining when I came in this morning."

"Not like this," Olivia insisted. "This sounds like it's only going to get worse, and you know what that could mean."

Cassidy nodded. "Yeah. Connor's going to be stomping around the ranch house, muttering that he can't do any of his work because it's raining too hard."

Olivia shook her head. Her intern was misreading the situation. "I think you should go home," she said.

Cassidy still saw no need for her evacuation. "To watch Connor stomping around?"

"No, to keep from being washed away," Olivia insisted. "You should know better than I do just how quick these flash floods can hit."

"I know," Cassidy agreed, "but there hasn't been one in a couple of years and even that one was over before it practically started." She waved away what she felt was Olivia's needless concern. "Besides, I can take care of myself."

Olivia sighed as she rolled her eyes. "Lord, did you ever pick the right profession. Someday, you are going to make one hell of a lawyer, but in order to do that, Cassidy, you're going to need to stay alive. Now, I might not be a native to this area, but I've seen what a flash flood can do—"

"I can swim," Cassidy insisted stubbornly.

"All well and good," Olivia replied patiently as she began to pack up some things on her desk, "but your truck can't. Now, I'm not going to spend the next hour arguing with you. I'm your boss and what I say goes. So now hear this—go home."

Cassidy retired her pen and the stack of papers she'd been going through with a sigh. "Okay, like you said, you're the boss."

Olivia smiled at her. "Yes, and I've been arguing a lot longer than you have. Although, given what your brother said to me at the wedding a few weeks ago, you were born arguing."

Cassidy paused to give her boss a penetrating look. "Which brother was that?" she asked conversationally.

Olivia wasn't being taken in for a moment. Finished packing her briefcase, she snapped the locks into place. Behind her, the wind and rain were rattling the window. "I never reveal my sources."

"Isn't that what a journalist usually says?"

"Where do you think they got it from?" Olivia asked with a smug smile. Packed, she rose from her chair. "I'm not sure if my kids can recognize me in the daylight. Although…" She glanced out the window again. The world outside the small, one-story building that housed her law firm had suddenly become shrouded in darkness. "There's not all that much daylight to be had, and it's getting scarcer by the minute."

Raising her voice, Olivia called out to her partner. "Cash, we're locking up."

The words were no sooner out of her mouth than the lights overhead went out.

"None too soon, if you ask me," Cash Taylor commented, poking his head into the office. "Is it just us," he asked, flipping the light switch off and on with no change in illumination, "or do you think the whole town's lost power?"

"Lord, I hope not," Olivia commented with feeling. "The only thing worse than cooking over a hot stove is *not* having a hot stove to cook over."

"You have a fireplace, don't you?" Cassidy asked as she gathered a selected stack of papers together so she could review them that evening.

As far as Olivia was concerned, a fireplace was good for one thing and one thing only. "Yes, but that's for cuddling in front of with my husband after the kids are asleep in bed."

Cassidy grinned at this human glimpse into her boss's life. "In a pinch, it can also be used for cooking dinner as long as you're not trying to make anything too elaborate."

"Elaborate?" Olivia echoed. "I'd just settle for it being passably edible."

Now that she thought of it, Olivia had never made any reference to a meal she'd taken pride in preparing. The woman's talents clearly lay in another direction.

"Maybe you should stop at Miss Joan's on your way home," Cassidy suggested tactfully.

Cash seconded the suggestion. "It'll give my step-grandmother something to talk about."

"No offense, Cash, and I obviously haven't known her nearly as long as either one of you have, but I've never known Miss Joan to ever be in need for something to talk about. She's everybody's go-to person when it comes to getting the latest information about absolutely *everything*."

There was a sudden flash of lightning followed almost immediately by an ominous crack of thunder, causing all of them to involuntarily glance up.

"Well, if we don't all get a move on, this rain just might turn nasty enough to give *everybody* something to talk about—provided they're able to talk and aren't under five feet of water," Cash observed.

With one hand at each of their backs, Cash ushered the two women out of the main office and toward the front door.

The moment she opened the front door, Olivia knew that she'd made the right call to have them leave early. The rain was coming down relentlessly.

It was the kind of rain that placed raising an umbrella against the downpour in the same category as tilting at windmills. Olivia turned up the hood on her raincoat. Cash did the same with his jacket. Cassidy had come in wearing her Stetson, a high school graduation gift from her oldest brother, Connor. She held on to it with one hand while pressing her shoulder bag with its newly packed contents against her with the other.

Locking up, Olivia turned away from the door. She was having second thoughts about her estimation of the rain's ferocity.

"Maybe you should come stay at our place," she suggested to Cassidy.

"And interfere with your plans for the fireplace? I wouldn't dream of it," Cassidy responded with a grin. "I'll be fine. See you in the morning, boss."

The rain seemed to only grow fiercer, coming down

at an angle and lashing at anyone brave enough to venture out of their shelter.

Taking two steps toward her vehicle, Olivia turned toward her intern. "Last chance!" she called out to Cassidy.

Rather than answer her, Cassidy just waved her hand overhead as she made a dash for her four-by-four. Reaching it, she climbed in behind the wheel and pulled the door closed behind her.

Utterly soaked, Cassidy sat for a moment, listening to the rain pounding on the roof of her vehicle. This really was pretty bad, she silently acknowledged. Half of her expected to see an ark floating by with an old man at its helm, surrounded by two of everything.

Well, she couldn't just sit here, she told herself. She needed to get home. Pulling the seat-belt strap up and over her shoulder, she tucked the metal tongue into the slot.

"I better get going before Connor and Cole come out looking for me," she murmured. Connor got antsy when he didn't have anything to do.

Starting her vehicle, Cassidy turned on her lights and put the manual transmission into Drive before she turned on the radio.

Apparently music wasn't going to be on the agenda that afternoon, Cassidy realized with a sigh. The reception was intermittent at best—and hardly that for the most part. When a high-pitch squawk replaced the song that kept fading in and out, Cassidy gave up and shut off the radio.

With the rain coming down even harder, she turned

the windshield wipers up to their highest setting. The blades all but groaned as they slapped against the glass, fighting what was turning out to be a losing battle against the rain.

Exercising caution—something, to hear them talk, that all three of her brothers seemed to believe she didn't possess—Cassidy reduced her speed to fifteen miles an hour.

Three miles out of town, her visibility went from poor to next to nonexistent.

At this rate, it would take her forever to get home, and the rain was just getting worse. She needed to hole up someplace until the rain subsided. Remembering an old, empty cabin she and the others used to play in as kids, Cassidy decided that it might be prudent to seek at least temporary shelter there until the worst of the rain let up.

The cabin was less than half a mile away.

If the rain *didn't* let up, she thought when the cabin finally came into view, then she would be stuck there for the duration of this downpour with nothing to eat except for the half consumed candy bar she had shoved into her bag.

Her stomach growled, reminding her that she had skipped lunch.

Leaning forward in her seat, she looked up at the sky—or what she could make out of it.

"C'mon, let up," she coaxed. "The forecast specifically said 'rain.' It didn't say a word about 'floods' or the end of the world."

Cassidy sighed again, even louder this time. She

held on to the steering wheel tightly as she struggled to keep her vehicle from veering off the trail. Ordinarily, veering off wouldn't have been a big deal, but just as Olivia had predicted, the rain had become ferocious, turning what was normally a tiny creek into a rapidly flowing river.

One wrong turn on her part, and her truck would be *in* that river.

And then, just when it seemed to be at its very worst, the rain began to let up, going from what had all the characteristics of becoming a full-blown monsoon to just a regular fierce downpour. Even so, Cassidy knew she needed to get her truck onto higher ground before she found herself suddenly stuck and unable to drive— or worse.

The cabin was still her best bet. From what she remembered—and she really hadn't paid all that much attention to this aspect when she was a kid—the cabin *was* on high ground.

Most likely not high enough to enable her to get a signal for her cell phone, she thought darkly. What that meant was that she wouldn't be able to call Connor to assure him that she was all right. As much as she talked about being independent and being able to take care of herself, she didn't like doing that to her big brother. Connor had been both mother and father to the rest of them for the last ten years. What that had entailed was giving up his own dreams of a college education and a subsequent career. He'd done it in order to become their guardian when their father died three days after Connor had turned eighteen.

While she was grateful to Connor for everything he had done and appreciated the fact that he cared about her and the others, she was equally convinced that Connor needed a family of his own—a wife and at least a couple of kids, if not more—to care for and to worry about.

About to turn her truck in order to get it to higher ground, Cassidy thought she saw something out of the corner of her eye. It was bobbing up and down in the swollen water.

She thought it was rectangular—and pink.

You're losing your mind, Cassidy silently lectured herself.

The next second, her body went rigid as she heard something.

She couldn't have just heard—

No, that was just her imagination, getting the better of her. That was probably just some animal making that sound. It couldn't have been—

A baby!

"Damn it," Cassidy bit out, "that couldn't be—" And yet, she really thought she heard a baby crying.

You're really letting your imagination run away with you, she silently lectured.

Even though she was convinced she was wrong, Cassidy knew she couldn't just shrug it off. She had to look again—just in case.

It wasn't safe to turn the truck on a saturated road. Cassidy did the only thing she could in order to give herself peace of mind.

She threw her truck into Reverse.

Driving backward as carefully as she was able, she watched the road to see if she could catch sight of the bobbing pink whatever-it-was.

And then, her eyes glued to her rearview mirror, Cassidy saw it.

She wasn't crazy; there *was* something bobbing up and down in the water. Something rectangular and, from what she could make out, it appeared to be plastic. A plastic tub was caught up in the rushing waters and, for some reason that seemed to defy all logic, it was still upright and afloat.

If that wasn't miraculous enough, Cassidy could have sworn that the baby she'd thought she'd heard was in the bobbing pink rectangular plastic tub.

With the truck still in Reverse, Cassidy stepped on the gas pedal, pushing it as far down as she dared and prayed.

Prayed harder than she ever had before.

Chapter Two

The rear of Cassidy's truck fishtailed, and for one long, heart-stopping moment, she thought the truck was going to slide straight down into the rushing floodwater.

Everything was happening at a blinding speed.

Cassidy wasn't sure just how she managed it, but somehow she kept the truck on solid ground. Not only that, but with her heart in her throat, she backed up the vehicle far enough so that it was slightly ahead of the approaching bobbing tub—all this while the four-by-four was facing backward.

She knew what she had to do.

If Cassidy had had time to think it through, she would have seen at least half a dozen ways that this venture she was about to undertake could end badly.

But there *wasn't* any time to think, there was only time to react.

Throwing open the door on the driver's side, Cassidy jumped out of the truck and hit the ground running—as well as sliding. The ground beneath her boots was incredibly slippery.

The rain was no longer coming down in blinding

sheets. Although it was still raining hard, she barely noticed it. All she noticed, all she *saw*, was the crying baby in the plastic tub. And all she knew was that if she couldn't reach it in time, the baby would drown.

It still might.

They very well could *both* drown, but Cassidy knew she had to do something, had to at least *try* to save the baby. Otherwise, if she played it safe, if she did nothing at all, she would never be able to live with herself. Choosing her own safety over the life of another—especially if that life belonged to a baby—was totally unacceptable to her.

Cassidy wasn't even aware of the fact that as she rushed to the water's edge and dove in, she yelled. Yelled at the top of her lungs the way she had when she and her brothers would engage in the all-too-dangerous, mindlessly death-defying games they used to play as children. The one that came to her mind as she dove was when they would catapult from a makeshift swing—composed of a rope looped around a tree branch—into the river below. Then the ear-piercing noise had been the product of a combination of released adrenaline and fearlessness. What prompted her to yell now as she dove into the water was the unconscious hope that she could survive this venture the way she had survived the ones in her childhood. Then she had been competing with her brothers—and Laredo. Now she was competing against the laws of nature and praying that she would win just one more time.

The water was strangely warm—or maybe it was that she was just totally numb to the cold. She only had

one focus. Her eyes were trained on the plastic tub and
its passenger as she fought the rushing water to cut the
distance between her and the screaming baby.

The harder she swam, the farther away she felt the
tub was getting.

Keeping her head above the water, Cassidy let loose
with another piercing yell and filled her lungs with as
much air as she could, hoping that somehow that would
help keep her alive and magically propel her to the baby.
There was absolutely no logical way it could help; she
only knew that somehow it had to.

WILL LAREDO HAD no idea what he was doing out here.
Ordinarily he wasn't given to following through on
dumb ideas, and this was definitely a lapse on his part.
For all he knew, the colt he was looking for could have
found his way back to the stable and was there now,
dry and safe, while he was out here on something that
could only be called a fool's errand.

It was just that when that bolt of lightning had
streaked across the sky and then thunder had crashed
practically right over the stable less than a minute later,
it caused Britches to charge right out of the stable and
through the open field as if the devil himself was after
him.

Seeing the colt flee, Will ran to his truck and took
out after it as if he had no choice.

Will knew it was stupid, but he felt a special con-
nection to the sleek black colt. Britches had been born
shortly after he'd returned to take over his late father's
ranch, and he'd felt that if he lost the colt, somehow,

symbolically, that meant he was going to lose the ranch—and wind up being the ne'er-do-well his father had always claimed he was destined to be.

It was asinine to let that goad him into coming out here, searching for the colt, when the weather conditions made it utterly impossible to follow the animal's trail. Any hoofprints had been washed away the second they were made.

Hell, if he didn't turn around right now, *he* would wind up being washed away, as well.

His best bet was to take shelter until the worst of this passed. These sorts of storms almost always came out of nowhere, raged for a short amount of time, did their damage and then just disappeared as if they'd never existed.

But right now, he was wetter than he could remember being in a very long time and he wanted to—

Suddenly, he snapped to attention. "What the hell was that?"

The yell he thought he heard instantly propelled him back over a decade and a half, to a time when estrangement and spirit-breaking responsibilities hadn't entered his life yet. A time when the company of friends was enough to ease the torment of belittling words voiced by a father who was too angry at the hand that life had dealt him to realize that he was driving away the only thing he *did* have.

There it was again!

Will hit the brakes with as much pressure as he dared, knowing the danger of slamming down too hard. He didn't feel like being forced to fish his truck out of this newly created rushing river. Opening the door, he strained to hear the sound that had caused him to stop his truck in the first place.

He waited in vain.

The howl of the wind mocked him.

He was hearing things.

"You don't belong out here anymore, Laredo," he said, upbraiding himself. "What the hell are you trying to prove by going out looking for a colt that probably has more sense than you do? Go home before you drown out here like some damn brainless turkey staring up at the sky during a downpour."

Disgusted as well as frustrated, Will leaned out to grab hold of the door handle—the wind had pushed the door out as far as it would go. Just as he began to pull it toward him, he heard it for a third time.

That same yell.

"Damn it, I'm *not* hearing things," he swore, arguing with himself.

Getting out of the truck, he squinted against the rain and looked out at the rushing water. Yesterday, this entire length of wet land hardly contained enough water to qualified being called a creek; now it was on its way to becoming a full-fledged raging river.

Will's square jaw dropped as he realized that he wasn't looking at debris being swept away in the center of the rushing water. It was some sort of washtub, a washtub with what looked to be a doll in it.

That wasn't a doll; that was a baby!

He was already running to the water's edge when his field of vision widened and he saw her. Saw that Cassidy was fighting against the current and was desperately trying to reach the baby.

It hit him like a punch in his gut.

That was what he'd heard!

He'd heard Cassidy screaming out that yell, the one that Cole had come up with so many summers ago. It had something to do with making them band together, giving them the strength of five instead of just one. They'd been kids then.

She wasn't a kid anymore and there were all sorts of things he wanted to yell at her now, all of them ultimately boiling down to the word *idiot*.

But that was *after* he got to her.

And before that could happen, he had to save Cassidy's damn fool hide. Hers and that baby she was trying to rescue.

Where the hell had it come from?

He had no time to try to figure that out now. Later, that was for later.

Will gave himself a running start, using the increasing speed he built up to propel him as he dove into the water.

He swam the way he never swam before—as if his life depended on it.

As if *her* life depended on it.

Hers and that baby's.

Divorcing himself from any other thoughts—from anger, fear, astonishment—Will focused entirely on the goal he'd just set for himself. Rescuing the woman who took special delight in filleting him with her tongue whenever the opportunity arose, and the baby he'd never seen before, both of whom had just one thing in common: they had absolutely no business being out here under these conditions.

And they had one more thing in common: both of them were going to die here if he didn't reach them in time.

HER ARMS WERE getting really, really heavy, but she knew that if she gave in to the feeling, gave in to the very thought of how exhausted she felt, both she and most likely this baby were not going to live to see another sunrise.

Hell, they weren't going to live to see another half hour if she didn't find a way to save them.

Her lungs aching so much that they hurt, she still somehow managed to tap into an extra burst of energy. She stretched out her arms as far as they would go with each stroke, and she finally managed to get close enough to the baby to just glide her fingertips along the lip of the tub.

C'mon, just a little farther, just a little farther, she frantically urged herself.

"Gotcha!" Cassidy cried in almost giddy triumph, her fingertips securing just the very rim of the tub. Her heart pounding madly, she pulled the tub to her. "I've got you, baby," she all but sobbed. "I've got you!"

The problem was, she'd used up all of her energy, and, while she'd finally, *finally* managed to reach the baby, both she and it were still in the middle of the rushing water.

The situation didn't exactly look hopeful.

And then Cassidy felt something snaking around her waist and holding her fast as it grabbed her from behind. Exhausted beyond belief, unable to turn to see what had caught her, Cassidy still frantically cast about for some way to free herself and the baby before whatever it was that was holding her dragged them down to the bottom of this newly formed river.

With no weapon within reach, Cassidy frantically pulled back her arm and struck hard at whatever was holding on to her with her elbow. Her only hope was to use the element of surprise to drive off whatever creature had ensnared her.

"Ow! Damn it, Cassidy, I should have my head examined for not letting you drown instead of trying to save you," the deep voice behind her grumbled.

She could *feel* the words as they rumbled out because the man behind her had such a tight hold on her; his chest was pressed up against her back closer than the label on a jar of jam.

"Laredo?" she cried, absolutely astonished even as she struggled to keep the very last ounce of energy from seeping out of her body. Confusion vibrated through her. "What the hell are you trying to do?"

"I thought that was rather obvious," he bit off coldly, both his breath and his words grazing the back of her head. "I'm trying to save you from drowning in this damn flash flood." Before she could offer any sort of a protest, he turned the tables on her. "What the hell are *you* doing out here?"

She had a death grip on the baby's tub, which in turn kept the baby from being swept away by the river.

"What does it look like I'm doing?" she challenged angrily.

"Proving me wrong," he answered, still keeping one arm firmly secured around her torso as he continued to slowly, powerfully, make his way back to the bank.

"Okay, I'm waiting," Cassidy retorted weakly, mentally bracing herself.

Whatever was coming was not going to be flattering. She knew him too well to expect anything else. She also knew him well enough to know he was bound to save her because of the same ingrained sense of honor they all shared.

"Why are you wrong?" she gasped when he didn't say anything.

"Because you *can* still find new ways to mess up, just when I thought you'd exhausted all the available possibilities."

Anger appeared out of nowhere, giving her an unexpected surge of energy. She knew it wouldn't last, so she talked quickly.

"There was a baby in the river. What was I supposed to do?" she demanded weakly. "Wave at it?"

"No, but drowning with it wasn't exactly going to help anything," Will snapped as he finally managed to reach the riverbank with both of them in tow.

The baby was still crying. It was loud enough to almost drown out the sound of their voices.

"I wasn't drowning," she informed him.

She meant to snap the answer at him, but all she could manage was an indignant gasp. Her last surge of energy was all but gone. But he had a way of making her so angry, she still felt compelled to argue.

"I had everything under control. I didn't need your help."

Exhausted himself from fighting against the current, Will fell back against the bank. It was still raining, but at this point, he was hardly aware of it.

"Right." The single word mocked her.

She would have peppered him with biting rhetoric if she only had the energy. As it was, taking in a full breath was about all she could manage. She couldn't remember *ever* being this exhausted.

The moment she had at least an ounce of extra energy to spare, she would direct it toward the baby whose cries had turned into subdued whimpers—and that, in reality, worried her more than the cries did.

So, for the moment, all she could say in response to Will as they both lay on the bank, getting wetter and silently grateful that neither one of them would become a statistic today in this latest battle with Mother Nature, was, "Thanks for the thought, though."

"Any time," he murmured.

In the distance, as the rain began to swiftly retreat, he could have sworn that he heard a horse whinnying.

Or maybe it was a colt.

His mouth curved ever so slightly.

Britches was safe after all.

Chapter Three

Cassidy hated to admit it, even if it was just to herself, but there was no getting away from it. Laredo had a great smile that warmed up a cold room and could easily set even the coolest heart on fire, at least momentarily. It was exactly for this reason why she would never even allow him to suspect that she felt this way.

Ever since she could remember, Will Laredo attracted the female of the species as if they were thirsty jackrabbits and he was the only watering hole for more than two hundred miles. Cody and Cole—and even Connor on occasion—seemed to think that was one of Laredo's attributes. She, on the other hand, viewed it in an entirely different light.

It just gave the man an even bigger head than he already had.

When she saw the corner of his mouth curve just now as they both lay on the bank, gasping for breath, all these other thoughts came crowding into her head. Like how this resembled the aftermath of a marathon lovemaking session with the two of them lying so close together, breathless and grateful.

She was delirious, she angrily upbraided herself.

Cassidy squelched her thoughts. She was exhausted and consequently—although she would have rather died right here on the spot than admit it—vulnerable. This was *definitely* not the time to have thoughts like that marching through her brain.

People did stupid things when they felt vulnerable—even her. Stupid things that would go on to haunt them for the rest of their lives.

Well, not her.

"What are you smiling about?" she demanded breathlessly, expecting him to say something about getting to play the superhero to her damsel in distress—or something equally irritating.

She braced herself to lash out and put him in his place.

But Laredo surprised her by saying, "Britches made it."

Britches? Her eyes narrowed into probing slits. Right now, the baby they had saved was quiet, and she was beyond grateful for that.

Was Laredo referring to the baby?

"Is that some kind of a nickname?" she challenged.

Was this yet another way to talk down to her? Even so, she had to admit that she was glad Laredo had showed up when he did. Despite her defensive words to the contrary, she really wasn't 100 percent convinced that she would have been able to make it back to the bank with the baby without Laredo's help.

But if she even hinted at that, he would never let her live it down.

"No, it's a name," Will told her mildly, "for my colt."

"Your colt?" she repeated.

Was he talking about his father's old gun? As she recalled, Jake Laredo had kept an old Colt .45 that he claimed had belonged to his great-great-grandfather, handed down to him by Stephen Austin, the man who'd founded the Texas Rangers. There was more to the story, but she'd always pretended to be disinterested whenever he mentioned it. In her opinion, Laredo's head was big enough. She didn't need to add to it by acting as if she cared about anything he had to say.

"A colt's a male horse under the age of four," he told her patiently.

Some of her energy had to be returning because she could feel her back going up. Heroic endeavors or not, Laredo was talking down to her again, Cassidy thought, annoyed.

"I know what a colt is," she snapped, or thought she did. Afraid of scaring the baby again, she lowered her voice. "I just didn't know you had one."

"It's a horse ranch," he reminded her, referring to the property that his father had left to him—something she was aware of since she was in Olivia Santiago's office when he'd been called in and told about his father's will. The fact that his father had left it to him had rendered Will speechless. She'd almost felt sorry for him—almost. "What else am I going to have?"

"Debts."

The answer came out before Cassidy could censor herself. It was Laredo's fault. He had that sort of effect on her. The next moment, remorse set in. He was the bane of her existence, but he didn't deserve that.

"Sorry," she mumbled, "I didn't mean to say that."

"Sure you did." Instead of being annoyed, he let her words pass. "Because it's true," he admitted matter-of-factly.

Everyone in town knew that his father had had money troubles. They'd only gotten worse over time. There was no reason to believe that anything had changed just before he died. Jake Laredo had sought refuge in the bottom of a bottle, drinking to the point of numbness, after which he'd pass out. Subsequently, the ranch had fallen into disrepair and ruin. When he'd gotten the letter from Olivia about his father's death, he'd returned only to put the old man into the ground. He'd been surprised that the ranch was still standing and that there were a couple of horses—rather emaciated at that—still in the stable.

Will saw it as a challenge.

"It's probably why he left the place to me," Will was saying, more to himself than to her. "It was his final way of sticking it to me."

Still lying on the bank, Cassidy turned her head toward him. She decided it had to be what she'd just gone through. The experience had to have rattled her brain to some degree because she was actually feeling sorry for Laredo—a little, she quickly qualified. But the feeling was there nonetheless.

"Someone else would just walk away," she pointed out to him.

"Someone else isn't me," he told Cassidy. "Besides,

I can't walk away. If I did, that old man would have the last laugh."

The last laugh would have meant that he couldn't do the honorable thing, couldn't pay off his father's debts, couldn't make a go of the ranch. In effect, it would have made him no better than Jake Laredo had been. Or at least that was the way Will saw it.

"I don't think he's laughing much where he is now," Cassidy said quietly.

Meaning hell, Will thought. He almost laughed at that but checked himself in time. "Well, I see you haven't lost it."

Her eyebrows drew together in a puzzled look. She was actually trying to be nice to the man. Served her right. What the hell was he talking about?

"Lost what?" she asked.

"That knack of saying the first thing that comes into your head without filtering it," he told her.

Cassidy had to admit that she felt more comfortable sparring with the cocky so-and-so, receiving stinging barbs and giving back in kind.

She could feel the adrenaline starting to rush through her veins again. She was definitely coming around, Cassidy thought.

"Hey," she cried, bolting upright as the realization suddenly hit her. "It's stopped raining."

"And that baby's stopped crying," Will added. "It's like Nature's taking a break."

The moment he said it, Cassidy's head snapped back around. What had struck her subconsciously now hit her head-on. Laredo was right; the baby in the tub was no longer crying.

Was that because…?

Her heart froze as she looked down at the infant in the tub again. And then she exhaled the breath she'd just sucked in and held a second ago.

Wonder of wonders, the baby was sleeping. For a moment, she'd thought the worst.

"I guess all that crying took everything out of him— or her," Cassidy added as an afterthought.

"Him or her? You don't know if it's a boy or a girl?" he asked her incredulously.

Rather than answer him directly, she said, "Well, it was crying so hard I couldn't think, so it's probably a male," she speculated.

He was trying to nail Cassidy down, something that had never been easy to do. "Then you've never seen this baby before?" he questioned.

"Well, I haven't been to the new-baby store recently, so no, I've never seen this baby before. Not until I saw it floating by in that flash flood that used to be a creek," Cassidy added.

Laredo looked at her skeptically, which indicated that he didn't believe her. But then, she supposed that just this once she couldn't really fault him. If she were in his place, she wouldn't have believed him, either.

"No, seriously, I've never seen this baby before." She looked at the sleeping infant and shook her head. The whole thing seemed almost macabre as well as incredible. "Who sticks a baby into a plastic tub?" she asked.

"Someone trying to save its life would be my guess,"

Will said, speculating. "Maybe it was someone who's new to the area. They were driving through and got caught up in the flash flood—this could have been their last-ditch attempt to save the baby."

She had a question for him. "Who drives around with a plastic tub in their car?"

"Someone who had no place to live," he guessed. The expression on her face told him that she thought he was stretching it. "Hey, I don't have all the answers, but it's a possibility."

"It's also a possibility that the kid's mother or father is looking for him or her right at this very minute," Cassidy said, thinking how she would feel in that person's place.

Scared out of her mind.

The baby began to stir. Any second it was going to wake up and start crying again, she thought, looking at the infant intently.

And then it was no longer a speculation.

The baby they had rescued was awake again. The next moment, it began to cry.

Will recalled something he'd overheard a young mother saying. "At this age, they only cry for a reason. It's either hungry or wet," he told her, getting up.

"Or maybe it just doesn't like being crammed in a little plastic tub." Speculation aside, she lifted the infant out of the confining tub. And as she did so, she also quickly drew back a section of the diaper and took a peek. "He's also wet," she pronounced, although that could have been the result of being caught up in the flood.

"He?" Will echoed as he stood up.

"He," Cassidy repeated. "It's a boy." Holding the baby to her chest, she started to get up only to have Will reach down for the infant. She tightened her hold. "What are you doing?"

"You don't want to risk falling over with the baby as you get up," he told her as if it was a common occurrence for her. "I'm already up."

"Good for you," Cassidy commented sarcastically. Grudgingly she let Will take the baby, then popped up right beside him and reached to take the child back.

But Will didn't release him. "What are you planning on doing?" he asked.

"Well, I certainly don't want to have a tug-of-war with this child if that's what you're thinking." It came out like an accusation.

Will didn't rise to the bait. "No, what I'm thinking is that this baby needs to be seen by one of the doctors at the clinic." It wasn't a suggestion.

Okay, Cassidy allowed, so maybe Laredo was capable of having a decent thought once in a blue moon. But she wasn't about to let him think that he'd gotten the jump on her.

"That's just where I'm taking him," she informed Will coolly.

But he wasn't budging.

Now what? she thought, exasperated.

"You planning on tossing him in the back of the truck?" Will asked.

Her eyebrows drew together like light blond thunderbolts, aimed right for his heart. "Of course not," she snapped.

He continued to hold on to the infant protectively. The baby was beginning to fuss. But Will's attention was focused on the woman who stood in his way. "Okay, then what?"

"Um—"

To Cassidy's surprise, he relinquished his hold on the infant, who was now beginning to cry. "C'mon, you hold the baby, I'll drive."

It really irked her when he took the lead this way, as if he was in control of everything, including her. "I don't need you to drive us."

Standing right in front of her, Will drew himself up to his full height. Although Cassidy would have never admitted it out loud, he did make a formidable obstacle.

"You planning on holding him in one arm while driving with the other hand?" he asked, then challenged, "On these roads?"

She knew he was right and hated giving him that. But unless she was willing to stand here, listening to the baby crying progressively louder—possibly even endangering this baby—she had no choice.

"Okay, fine," she bit out, "*you* drive—but we're coming back for my truck."

He nodded absently. "I've got no problem with that," he said, leading the way back to his vehicle.

"What's that supposed to mean?" Cassidy asked.

He made her crazy. It felt as if everything out of his mouth came with a hidden meaning. Plus, Cassidy found she had to really lengthen her stride in order to try to keep up with him. But there was no way she was going to ask Laredo to slow down. She'd never done it with any of her brothers—all of whom were taller than she was—and she sure as hell wasn't going to do it with Laredo.

Instead, Cassidy glared at the back of his head all the way to his truck.

When they reached it, Will opened the door directly behind the driver's seat and held it open for her.

She immediately took it to mean he regarded her as subservient to him. "What's wrong with the front seat?" she asked.

Will continued to hold the door open for her. "Backseat's safer for the baby."

Cassidy blew out a breath. Damn it, Will was right, and she hated that.

When he took hold of her elbow, she pulled free and nearly jabbed him with it. "I can get into the truck on my own."

Unfazed, Will said, "I'm just looking out for the baby."

Cassidy scowled at him. "Just because you *helped* save him doesn't automatically make you his fairy godmother."

"I kind of see myself more like a guardian angel than a fairy godmother," he deadpanned. "They've got bigger wings." He added that with a sly wink that made her desperately want to punch him if only her arms weren't full.

Cassidy bit her bottom lip to keep from saying something caustic. The next moment, as she seated herself directly behind the driver's seat, she felt Laredo reaching over her.

So much for silence, she thought, giving up. "Okay, what the hell do you think you're trying to do?" Cassidy demanded.

"I *think* I'm trying to get this seat belt around you and the baby. We're liable to hit a skid in this weather, and I don't want the two of you suddenly flying out the window—or worse," he added with deliberate emphasis.

"Since when did you become so damn thoughtful?" Cassidy asked coldly.

Her eyes widened. Was it her imagination, or had Laredo's hand just slid over her lap as he stepped back after fastening the seat belt?

"I've always been thoughtful, Cassidy. You've just been too mean-tempered to notice," he answered mildly.

Before she had a chance to snap at him, Will shut her door and went over to get into the front seat.

"I am *not* mean-tempered," she informed him, struggling to hold on to that same temper.

Will shut the door and secured his own seat belt before starting the vehicle. Only then did he raise his eyes to the rearview mirror to look at her. "I've got a town full of people who might argue with you about that," he replied mildly.

Her eyes met his in the mirror. She could feel her temper heating, but there was no time to give Laredo a piece of her mind or take him down. The baby had begun to cry in earnest now. Even if the infant was just wet and hungry, she had no dry clothes, diapers or food to offer him, so the sooner they got to the clinic, the better.

"Just drive!" she ordered.

"Yes, ma'am," Will responded.

She didn't need to see his face to know that his mouth had assumed that all-too-familiar smirk she knew and hated. She could hear it in his voice.

Okay, Laredo. I need you to help me get this baby to the medical clinic. But once we do and this little guy is someone else's problem, I am going to become your worst nightmare.

She paused for a moment, savoring that thought. And anticipating.

Even worse than I already am.

Chapter Four

The infant hadn't stopped crying since before they'd gotten into the vehicle. The wailing noise was making it hard for Will to think. That, added to the fact that the rain had picked up again, was enough to really put him on edge.

"You sure he's not hurt?" Will asked, glancing at Cassidy over his shoulder.

She raised her eyes to meet his.

"I have no idea, but I know that he will be if you keep taking your eyes off the road like that. It's starting to rain harder again," Cassidy pointed out. Her nerves were getting the better of her.

"Gee, really?" Will asked, feigning surprise. "I hadn't noticed."

He hated the way Cassidy treated him, as if he was totally oblivious to things. She'd done that for as far back as he could remember, and at times he had to admit it almost amused him. But right now, with the baby crying and the roads growing progressively more hazardous, he was having a rough time staying calm.

Although he did his best to pretend otherwise, no one

could get to him the way Cassidy could. There was just something about the way she talked, the way she tossed her head, the smug, superior gleam in her eyes, that just made him want to get back at her and teach her a lesson.

Just what form that lesson would take he hadn't worked out yet. But if he was going to remain in Forever, even for a little while, he had a feeling that day would come—and most likely sooner than either one of them reckoned, most of all her.

"That doesn't surprise me," Cassidy told him, acting as if she'd taken his words at face value. "But do us all a favor and try to pay attention. I've got way too many things to do to die out here with you today."

He laughed shortly. "Funny, I was thinking the same thing."

"Funny," she said, mimicking his voice, "I didn't know you *could* think."

He'd almost reached the end of his supply of patience. "You really want to get into this now?" Will asked, his voice becoming ominous and foreboding.

"What I *want*," Cassidy informed him, "is to get into town while I still have any hearing left." She'd tried everything in her rather limited arsenal of tricks with this baby—rocking him, trying to talk to him, patting his back—all to no avail. "How can something so little make such a loud noise?"

Will focused his attention back on the road—just in time to avoid driving into a large branch that had broken off a nearby tree. Another casualty of the storm.

Heart pounding, he drove around it. "Maybe his crying like that is a good thing. At least it means he's got healthy lungs."

Laredo was doing it again, she thought. Acting like a know-it-all. He wasn't here in the backseat with the baby blowing out *his* eardrums. "Where did you get your degree, Dr. Laredo?"

"Same place you learned to be a shrew—no, wait, you just came by that naturally, didn't you?"

Okay, she'd had enough, Cassidy thought. "Stop the truck," she ordered.

Thinking that something was seriously wrong, Will did as she asked. His thoughts immediately zeroed in on the baby.

"Why? What's wrong?" he asked, twisting in his seat.

They were right on the outskirts of Forever. The clinic wasn't all that far off. Rain or no rain, she could walk from here.

Cassidy began to undo her seat belt. "I can't listen to you blathering on like this. I can walk to the clinic from here."

Biting off a curse, Will started the vehicle again. Gravity had Cassidy falling back in her seat. Because she'd inadvertently squeezed him, the baby was wailing even harder than he had been before.

"Damn you, Laredo," she cried. "What the hell do you thinking you're doing *now*?"

"Driving a crazy woman and the baby she's holding to the clinic," he bit out. "Now shut up and hold on."

She didn't want to give him the satisfaction of thinking that she was obeying, but by the same token, she didn't want to get into another fight with him when he was this angry already. So she did as he told her.

She really didn't have any other choice.

Cassidy remained in the truck and counted off the minutes in her head until they reached the clinic.

Rather than park the truck in the lot—which was the emptiest he could remember ever seeing it since he'd returned to Forever—Will parked directly in front of the medical clinic's front door.

Just in time, he judged.

Daniel Davenport, the doctor who had reopened the clinic when he'd arrived in Forever several years ago, was just locking up.

"Hey, Doc," Will called out, raising his voice in order to be heard above the crying baby and the howling wind. "Got time for one more?"

Dan turned. For the first time since he'd begun to run the clinic, the facility was entirely empty. He'd sent his partner and the two nurses who worked with them home over half an hour ago. Just in case someone did come by, he'd hung back, giving it another half hour.

Thirty minutes had come and gone. He wanted to get home to his family. Dan figured there was no point in waiting any longer. But obviously there was, he thought, looking from the man who'd just called out to him to the young woman who was emerging out of Will's somewhat battered truck holding what appeared to be an infant in her arms.

Dan caught himself thinking that they were as unlikely a couple as he had ever seen. For the most part, Dan was oblivious to most of the gossip and the personal details that made the rounds at gathering places like Miss Joan's Diner and Murphy's Saloon. His attention was exclusively focused on helping and healing the people who sought him out at the clinic.

But even *he* knew that whenever the newly returned Will Laredo and Cassidy McCullough were within spitting distance of each other, they usually did. Neither could keep their temper holstered, especially not Cassidy.

His eyes narrowed slightly as they focused on the smallest player in this group. There was no way in God's green earth that baby was theirs.

"Caught me just in time," Dan said, addressing Will as he unlocked the door he had just locked. Pocketing the key, Dan pushed the door opened with the flat of his hand. "I take it that 'one more' you're referring to is the baby?"

"It is," Will answered.

"Where did you find it?" Dan asked, ushering in the trio. He didn't waste time asking if the infant belonged to either one of them. He knew it couldn't.

"Bobbing up and down in the creek, except it was more like a rushing river at the time," Cassidy told him.

Once inside, she pushed back her wet hair and turned to face the doctor. "I'm thinking of calling him Moses," she quipped, looking down at the squalling baby, "since I pulled him out of the river."

"More like out of a rubber tub in the river," Will corrected.

"Okay, maybe you think we should call him Rubber Ducky," Cassidy retorted sarcastically, turning to glare at Will.

"Back up. The baby was in a rubber *tub*?" Dan questioned, looking from one to the other, waiting for enlightenment.

Cassidy nodded. "It was probably the only floatation device his mother—"

"Or father—" Will pointedly interjected. Although he had enjoyed neither, he knew by watching the McCulloughs that parental feelings were not the exclusive domain of the female population.

Cassidy ignored him and continued with her narrative "—could find. It was obvious that she was trying to save him."

"Then you didn't find either of the baby's parents?" Dan asked, again looking from Cassidy to Will for an answer.

Cassidy shook her head. "I just saw the baby—and almost missed seeing him at first. He was in the middle of the rushing water, crying." She winced as a particularly loud cry pierced the air right next to her ear. "Kind of like he is now. Could you check him out, please?" She held out the infant to Dan. "See if there's something wrong with him. I'll pay for it," she quickly added, not wanting the doctor to think that just because the baby wasn't related to her that she expected him to do the examination for free.

"I'll take care of it, Doc," Will assured him. Finances were tight, thanks to what he'd found himself walking into when he took over his father's ranch, but he still had a little cash to work with if he did some artful juggling.

"I'm not worried about that right now," Dan told both of them.

When he'd first arrived to reopen the clinic in Forever, Dan had viewed it as a temporary assignment until another doctor could be found to take over the practice on a more permanent basis. But even then, monetary compensation had never been his goal.

What he hadn't counted on was the emotional rewards that went along with this job.

"While I'm giving this little guy the once-over, one of you should call the sheriff and tell him about what happened," Dan suggested. "Could be his parents are stranded somewhere right now and need some rescuing themselves."

Will's eyes shifted toward Cassidy, and she could hear the question as if he'd said it out loud.

"I didn't see anyone. That doesn't mean they weren't there," she admitted, then frowned. "But it could also mean that they could be dead." Cassidy thought for a moment. "Last really bad flash flood we had, Warren Brady's nephew pulled his car up on the side of the road and got caught in it before he even knew what was happening. He was gone before anyone could reach him, and that was in a matter of moments."

Dan sighed. He hated hearing about senseless losses like that. It made him that much more determined to do as much as he could for those he *could* help.

"This is going to take a while," he told the two people in his waiting room. "Why don't you wait out here until I can determine if this little guy's got a problem beyond missing parents?"

It wasn't so much a question as politely voiced instruction.

Will nodded toward the phone on the reception desk. "Mind if I use your phone to call the sheriff?" he asked Dan. "I can't seem to get any reception on my cell phone. The storm wreaked havoc on the signal."

"Go right ahead. I'll be back when I'm finished with the exam." The baby let loose with another lusty wail. Dan glanced toward Cassidy, an amused smile on his face. "Sure sounds like he's got a healthy set of lungs on him, though," he noted with a laugh.

She didn't have to look in his direction to know that Laredo had a smug expression on his face. Just like she knew he was going to rub it in.

She didn't have to wait long.

"Told you," Will said, clearly vindicated.

Cassidy had no intention of going down without a fight. "Even a broken clock is right twice a day," she pointed out.

"Set your standards that high, do you?" Will asked with a smile as he began to tap out the sheriff's number on the phone's keypad.

Cassidy curled her fingers into her hands to keep from grabbing the first thing she could find to throw at Laredo's head. If she was going to kill him, she knew she would have to do it when there were no witnesses around. And if she gave Laredo what was coming to him, she knew that Dan would come out to see what the noise was all about.

Restless, agitated, not to mention concerned about

the infant she'd rescued, instead of sitting, Cassidy paced around the waiting room.

Well, this day wasn't going the way she'd thought it would when she'd gotten up this morning, she thought in frustration. She'd planned on getting a number of things done in the office today. She was really determined to prove herself an asset to Olivia.

Instead, here she was, killing time in the clinic's waiting room, sharing space with Will Laredo of all people.

Why did both of them need to stay here, waiting for the doctor to give them the results of his examination? Laredo had two ears, she thought. At the very least, he could hear whatever it was that Dan had to say. Meanwhile, she could—

She could wait right here, she thought darkly. Her truck was still out where she'd left it. As much as she hated to admit it, she needed Laredo to drive her back to it.

Cassidy blew out a frustrated breath. More than anything else, she hated being backed into a corner like this.

Damn it, maybe if she called one of her brothers?

Out of the corner of her eye, she saw Laredo holding out the phone receiver to her. She eyed him quizzically. Couldn't he talk?

And then he did.

"Sheriff wants to talk to you," Will said.

She made no move to take the receiver. "Why?"

"Do you have to question everything I say?" he asked, annoyed.

There was as close to an innocent look in her eyes as possible as she replied, "Yes."

Laredo did what he could to hang on to the last of his composure and told her in carefully measured words, "He's got a couple of questions."

"What did you tell him?"

Will never missed a beat. "That you're a royal pain, but he wants to talk to you, anyway." With that he pushed the receiver toward her again.

Cassidy took it grudgingly. But when she spoke, nothing but pure honey dripped from her lips. Will entertained thoughts of strangling her.

"Hello? Sheriff? This is Cassidy McCullough. Laredo said you wanted to ask me something."

"Hi, yes. Will said you were the first one to dive into the floodwater to save this baby you saw."

Well, at least Laredo hadn't made himself the hero of the little drama—but then, in her heart, she knew he wouldn't have. He wasn't like that around other people. It was only when they were together that he went out of his way to drive her insane and contemplate justifiable homicide with every breath she took.

"Yes, I was," she answered.

"Did you see any other vehicle around, on either side of the rising water, or *in* the water?" Rick Santiago asked.

She was completely honest with him. "I really wasn't looking for another vehicle," Cassidy admitted. "But as far as I remember, nothing else caught my eye. It looked like the baby was alone."

"And it was in a plastic tub? Did I hear Will right?" Rick questioned uncertainly.

No matter how many times she said it or heard it, Cassidy had to admit that it still sounded weird. "Yes. Like the kind they give you when you get discharged from a hospital. Maybe the mother had just come home from the hospital. Or maybe she was a nurse," she added suddenly as the thought occurred to her.

"More likely the patient," Rick said in speculation. Although at this point, anything was possible. "Exactly where was this?"

A product of the area, Cassidy gave the sheriff the location as close to where she first saw the baby as she could, given that she'd been entirely focused on saving the baby and that some of the road she'd traveled on had been traversed backward in order to get parallel with the infant's makeshift sailing vessel.

She gave the sheriff every detail she could remember, holding nothing back.

"Okay, that helps," Rick commented when she was finished. "I'll have Joe and Cody check it out."

"Sheriff?"

He'd been about to hang up. It took him a second to respond. "Yes?"

"What happens to the baby if you can't find his parents?"

"Well, these aren't the best conditions and who knows how long that baby was out there, so locating his parents might be very difficult."

"And if it's impossible?" she pressed. "If you can't locate either of his parents, what happens to him then?"

"Someone would have to take him to Mission Ridge," Dan said grimly. "That's the closest social services office in the county."

"Oh." Everyone viewed social services as the last resort. For the most part, the people in Forever found a way to take care of their own, no matter how distant that match was. "Okay. Let me know if you find anything."

Disturbed, Cassidy frowned as she hung up. It only occurred to her after she'd replaced the receiver in the cradle that she'd forgotten to say goodbye.

The conversation had upset her that much.

Chapter Five

"Something wrong?"

Cassidy realized that Will was asking her a question, and from the sound of his voice, this wasn't the first time.

"Sorry. For a moment, I forgot you were here." Not wanting to seem as if he'd caught her off guard, she added, "Best moment of my life." An exasperated expression came over his face. Okay, he'd just expressed concern. Maybe she should have gone easier on him. She flashed a grin. "Sorry, couldn't help myself."

"We do seem to bring out the worst in each other," he commented. "Why do you think that is?"

Because everything you do rubs me the wrong way. And because sometimes just having you this close is way too crowded for me.

"Oh, I don't know," she said out loud. "You have a good moment every now and then."

Rather than say anything in response, Will went to the bay window and looked outside.

He'd aroused her curiosity. Had something outside caught his eye?

"What are you looking at?" Cassidy asked, joining him.

Will took his time answering her, making her wait. He figured she owed it to him. "You said something nice to me. I figure The Four Horsemen of the Apocalypse should be riding up the street anytime now, signaling the end of the world."

Cassidy slanted a glare at him. "Very funny. I had no idea you had a sense of humor."

Will pinned her with a penetrating look. The kind that went clear down to her bones. "You don't know a lot of things about me."

Although she'd never backed away from going toe-to-toe with him, there was something about standing close enough to feel his breath on her face that Cassidy found completely unnerving.

"And we're keeping it that way," she announced glibly, turning away.

"Round two," Will muttered, then shrugged. "Okay, have it your way."

"What other way is there?" Cassidy asked, knowing this would antagonize him. Then, just to drive her point home, she raised her chin, silently daring him to make some kind of a response.

She was deliberately goading him, and she knew it.

Damn it, what was it about this blond-haired witch that pulled him in like this? If he had a lick of sense, he'd just turn his back on her and be done with it. Yet here he stood, smack in the middle of her war zone.

It had to be some sort of insanity, like when a salmon

felt compelled to swim upstream to mate even though death lay waiting for it just beyond that finish line.

"Someday," Will warned her quietly, his voice barely a low growl, "you're going to find out."

Her chin rose a fraction of an inch higher as she smugly asked, "And you think you're going to be the one to show me?"

She was challenging him, and he knew he should either put her in her place with a couple of choice words or, better yet, just ignore her because he had a gut feeling that got to her more than anything.

But it was hard to ignore that face and that mouth when they were right in front of him like this.

Taunting him.

Daring him.

Before he could think his actions through—something he had *always* been able to do, even in the worst moments, even when his father would push him almost beyond the brink—Will caught hold of Cassidy by her shoulders.

His eyes searched her face, trying to understand the woman who was driving him crazy. Trying to get underneath the layers.

"You don't even have the sense to be afraid, do you?" he asked incredulously.

"Afraid?" Cassidy echoed, even as her heart did a quick little summersault that she damned herself for. "Why? You can't throw me off a cliff because we're standing on flat ground. And you can't strangle me because the doctor's just one scream away."

"You're right. I can't throw you off a cliff—whatever

the hell that means." What went through her mind, anyway? He didn't begin to have a clue. "And I can't strangle you."

"See?" Her eyes challenged him as she tossed her head again. "Nothing to be afraid of," she declared, as if she'd proved her point.

It was that smug look that came over her face that was her undoing, because it got to him as surely as if he'd just been shot straight through the heart with an armor-piercing bullet.

Before he knew what he was doing, still holding on to her shoulders, Will pulled her almost a full inch off the floor.

And then he kissed her.

It was meant to put her in her place and to frighten her.

What it did, instead, was frighten the hell out of him.

Frightened him because he didn't stop kissing her. He continued. Continued kissing Cassidy as he gradually allowed her feet to touch the floor, gradually leaned further into the kiss and found her responding to it.

At the same time, a whole host of things suddenly went off within him, things he couldn't put into words. The closest he could describe it was that it felt like someone had thrown a match into a shed full of Fourth of July fireworks.

ROCKETS WENT OFF EVERYWHERE.

Cassidy found herself melting like candle wax even as something in her head screamed, *This could be very dangerous!*

It wasn't screaming that because he was kissing her but because she was *responding* to his kissing her. Responding with every single part of her in a way she had *never* done before.

Other words failed to form in her head as sensations she couldn't begin to describe suddenly sprang up and mushroomed within her, scrambling for a foothold, desperately searching for more even as a part of her viewed the entire episode in mounting horror, as if she was watching some sort of a disaster movie unfold on the screen, all happening to someone else.

The last shred of what could only be termed as survival instincts finally rose and had her wedging her hands against his chest in a desperate bid to create some small sliver of space.

Or maybe what she actually felt was *Laredo* pulling back.

For the life of her, she couldn't distinguish which of them had made the first move to pull apart or begin to understand why such a feeling of bereavement was washing over her.

Cassidy's eyes blazed like blue flames as she ground out, "I should kill you."

"Don't bother," he told her coldly. "I think I'm already dead."

Why else, Will silently asked himself, would he have gone on kissing her that way? As if he wanted to. As if he couldn't draw another breath if he didn't.

It didn't make sense.

Before she could say anything else to him, coherent or otherwise, she heard Dan clearing his throat behind them. Her head all but swiveled as she turned to see who it was and realized that the doctor was standing right behind them.

Had Dan just walked in, or had he been there long enough to see what had just happened?

What *had* just happened? she silently demanded in complete confusion.

And why had she *let* it happen?

The expression on Dan's face gave her no answers. He looked as if he was taking this whole incident in stride. She certainly couldn't, she thought, irritated and disoriented.

"You'll be happy to hear that the baby is none the worse for his joyride on the floodwater this morning," Dan told both of them.

Will appeared mystified. "Then why was he crying like that?"

Dan lifted a shoulder in a casual shrug and then let it drop. "The usual reason babies this age cry. He was hungry and wet. Very wet." Dan laughed softly. "I've had patients who sounded a lot worse when they were hungry and wet. I changed him after my exam. We've got some spare baby clothes just for these occasions. And I fed him, as well. He seems rather happy now." Since Will was closer to him, he looked to him for an answer. "What's the status with his parents? Did the sheriff say anything?"

"I called it in, and the sheriff said he was sending out a couple of his deputies to look around, see if they can locate either one of the baby's parents, or find any sign of an abandoned vehicle."

Dan nodded. "Guess that's the best we can hope for now." And then he looked at the duo in front of him, as if he was waiting for one of them to speak up. When neither did, the doctor took the lead again. "Seeing as we don't have the parents yet, which one of you are going to take the baby?"

Cassidy blinked, feeling a little confused. "Take him where?"

"Well, home would be my first guess. I'd take him home with me, but Tina called a little while ago to say that one of the kids was running a fever. I wouldn't feel good about bringing this little guy into that kind of atmosphere. After what he's gone through, his resistance might be down," he explained in case they weren't following his argument. "It's not something I'd want to test."

"No, you're right," Will agreed. There was nothing to do but step up. He didn't even hesitate. "I guess since I rescued him, he's my responsibility."

That was all she needed to hear. "What d'you mean, *you* rescued him?" Cassidy cried. Did he think he could just dismiss her out of hand like this? As if she'd been some sideline observer?

"Okay," Will amended patiently. Then to her great outrage she heard him say, "Technically I rescued both of you."

Cassidy's mouth dropped open as she glared at him. "What?"

He did his best to hold back a few of the more choice words that rose to his lips. Instead, he reworded his previous statement.

"I rescued you rescuing him, does that suit you?" he asked.

"What would suit me is if you—"

When he'd gotten his medical degree, Dan had never thought that he was going to need one in mediation, as well.

"I think what we're all forgetting here is that this little guy needs a place to stay," Dan told them calmly, forcing their attention back to the baby. "So one of you decide which of you it's going to be—now."

"I'll take him," Cassidy announced. And then, as she heard herself say the words, she glared at Laredo and was forced to incline her head, grudgingly giving the man his due. He was better than she'd thought. "You planned it this way, didn't you?"

The expression on Will's face mimicked pure innocence.

"Don't know what you mean," Will responded. The look in his eyes told her otherwise.

Cassidy forced her thoughts to center on the baby she'd pulled out of the rushing water. And she remembered the drawer that her brother Cody had improvised to use as a bed for the baby he'd helped deliver a while back. The one he'd wound up bringing to the ranch, along with the baby's mother, Devon. Devon, Layla and Cody had gone on to form a family.

Cassidy abruptly shut down that line of thinking. This wasn't like that.

There was only one important thing to be gleaned from all this. The baby the doctor was holding in his arms looked as if he would have no trouble fitting into that drawer—at least until the baby's parents could be found or someone could come up with an alternate plan for this little nomad.

"Well, at least I have somewhere I can put him for the time being," Cassidy told the doctor. She spared Will what amounted to a dismissive glance. "Knowing you, you'd probably put him in the feed bin."

Instead of responding, Will looked at the doctor. "See what I have to put up with, Doc?"

But Dan quickly shook his head. "Oh, no, I'm not getting in the middle of this," he told both parties adamantly. "My only concern right now is to find a place for this little guy right here."

Cassidy spoke up and reminded the doctor, "I said I'd take him."

He waited a moment for her to back down. When she didn't, Dan nodded. "All right. I can give you some formula to take with you. I heard that the general store was closing down for the day, hoping to avoid the worst of the storm's damage."

He glanced from Will to Cassidy. "By the way, either of you have a name for him? I realize it's just temporary until we find his parents, but I need at least a first name to put down on my records, and I've always thought that 'Baby Boy Doe' sounds incredibly sad."

Will looked at the infant's face for a long moment. "How about Adam? Seems kind of fitting if you ask me—unless you've got some kind of an objection against it," he stated, looking pointedly at Cassidy.

She managed to surprise both him and Dan when she shook her head and said, "No, actually, I think that's kind of a nice name. 'Moses' was never really going to work," she added, referring to the name she'd first pinned on the baby.

"Well, Adam," Dan said, addressing the child in his arms, "I think you and I have just witnessed history being made. I don't recall hearing that these two *ever* agreed on anything before. Looks like you just might be having a good influence on them, what do you think?" He asked the baby as if it was a serious question.

Will glanced in her direction before saying, "Kind of nice, isn't it?"

There it was again, that damn sexy grin of his, she thought angrily. And now—heaven help her—she had something else to couple it with: that mind-blowing, toe-curling kiss of his, which was every bit as earth-shaking as all his female conquests claimed it was. And she was *never* going to give him the satisfaction of letting him know her reaction to either.

Not even on her deathbed.

So, retreating to form, Cassidy blew out a breath as she tossed her head again, doing her best to revert to a smug expression.

"Yeah, well, don't get used to it. I really doubt it's ever going to happen again because, odds are, you're not going to say anything smart again for a really, really long time."

"Okay, you two call a truce, and see about getting this baby to your ranch," Dan instructed Cassidy, "before this storm decides that it's not through with us yet." So saying, the doctor handed the baby to her. "I'll get that formula for you and a few disposable diapers as well until the general store opens again, hopefully tomorrow. Last I heard, it intended to open again in the morning."

Turning toward Will, Dan asked, "You want to come with me and help bring out those supplies?"

"Sure." He glanced in Cassidy's direction. "You'll wait?"

He didn't put anything past her, no matter what he assumed was the logical course of action. Cassidy and logic were hardly ever on good terms.

"Where am I going to go?" she asked. "You're my ride—at least until you get me back to my truck."

"I know that—but with you I'm never sure just what you're going to do," he told her honestly. "You just might get it into that fool head of yours to show me just how independent you are and suddenly set out on your own."

Cassidy pressed her lips together as she glared at him. She even glared at the back of his head as Will followed the doctor to the rear of the clinic.

"Do you two ever stop?" Dan asked wearily.

"I would if she would," Will responded.

"Then in other words, no," Dan concluded. Shaking his head, he laughed softly to himself.

"What's so funny?" Will asked as the doctor unlocked a couple of cabinets in the storage area.

"Oh, nothing," Dan said dismissively. And then he surprised the hell out of Will when he said, "Just picturing the wedding, and the aftermath."

Will's eyes had grown huge. "Whose wedding?"

Dan decided that, for now, he'd said enough.

Opening the cabinet door in the first exam room, he took out a supply of disposable diapers he kept on hand for his littlest patients. After stacking them on the exam table, he took out several cans of formula as well, plus a blanket. He put them all into a sack and handed it to Will.

"This should be enough to last Cassidy for at least a couple of days. By then, maybe she can get some from the store, or if that's still closed, Cody's wife might be able to spare some," the doctor suggested.

"This is more than generous, Doc," Will told him. Rather than argue with the doctor, which he knew Dan was wont to do if he raised the point about payment again, Will discreetly left a twenty on the exam table when he took the bag Dan gave him and then followed the doctor out of the room. It didn't begin to cover everything, but for now, it was all he could spare.

Chapter Six

"Ready to go?" Will asked Cassidy as he walked back into the reception area directly behind the doctor.

Cassidy was slowly pacing the room, gently rocking the baby in her arms and hoping that the ongoing motion would continue to keep him quiet and calm. She'd taken care of Cody's little girl on several occasions, but she felt way over her head right now—and was determined not to show it.

"Oh, more than ready," she answered.

Will nodded. "Okay, just let me load these baby survival supplies into the truck, and then I'll come back for the two of you," he told her. The next moment, he walked out of the clinic.

"Well, this has to be a first," Dan commented, almost more to himself than to the other adult occupant in the room.

Cassidy looked in the doctor's direction. "What is? A possibly homeless baby?"

Dan shook his head, his eyes crinkling in amusement. "No, you and Will working together."

Given her feelings toward Laredo, Cassidy was not

about to admit to something like that. "We might just be occupying the same space, Doc, and we might have the same general goal. But I guarantee that we are not 'working' together."

"There, that's what I mean," Dan told her. "Everyone in Forever is accustomed to seeing the two of you at odds with each other the second you're within in the same half-mile radius. But this—" he nodded at the dozing baby she was holding "—is bringing out something different from the two of you than your normal mode of behavior."

Dan had always been very nice to her and her family. The man probably didn't have a mean bone in his body, so she didn't want to pay him back by offending him. But she really found it difficult to go along with his view of what was going on.

"Yes, well, as soon as Laredo gets me back to my truck, life will go back to normal again," she promised with a little too much conviction.

Dan heard her out and smiled. "You go right on thinking that, Cassidy."

She raised her chin, the way she always did when she anticipated a fight, or at least an argument. "I will, because it's true." Because she didn't want to come off as combative with the doctor, she decided to redirect his attention toward something far more important than some artificial truce between her and Laredo. "How old do you think Adam is?"

He looked at the boy, quickly reviewing the exam in his mind. "Best guess is about two to three months old."

"And you've never seen him and his mother or father before?" Cassidy pressed. After all, a lot of patients came through this clinic every day. How could he remember every one of them?

But looking at the baby's face, Dan shook his head. "No, I'm afraid not."

"Maybe Dr. Alisha saw them?" she suggested. Granted, a few people did pass through Forever now that there was a hotel in town, but if they did, they did it during the summer months, not this time of year. It was nearing the end of November; nobody came here in the winter.

"It's not that big an office," Dan pointed out, looking down at the sleeping baby. "I would have recalled seeing this little guy and his mother or father if they ever came in here."

"Well, if you don't recognize him, I guess Adam and his parents were just passing through," Cassidy decided.

"There's another possibility," Will stated as he came back into the clinic. He was almost directly behind Cassidy.

She almost jumped. She hated when Will caught her off guard like that. "Okay, what?" she asked, sparing him a disdainful glance.

Will addressed his answer to the doctor rather than to her. "It's possible that he could be from the reservation. They've always had their own way of dealing with things. If this little guy was born on the reservation, there would have been no reason for you to have ever seen him or his mother before."

They all knew that the residents of the reservation rarely sought out the doctors at the clinic. They did on occasion, but those occurrences were few and far between. Nothing short of an outbreak of some sort of contagious disease brought the reservation residents to the clinic, seeking the help of the medical staff.

As if to contradict Will's theory, Cassidy pointed out, "He has blue eyes."

"Maybe one of Adam's parents wasn't Native American. Who knows?" Will looked at Cassidy. She was stubborn to a fault, and what she was the most stubborn about was admitting that he might be right. "It wouldn't hurt to ask around."

Cassidy frowned. She supposed Laredo might have a point. If anyone else had suggested that possibility, she would have readily agreed. But every word out of Will's mouth just seemed to irritate her beyond belief.

She pulled the blanket a little tighter around the baby.

"I'll mention it to Cody when I see him," she said dismissively. And then, glancing over her shoulder at Dan just before she left, Cassidy said, "Thanks again for everything, Doc."

"That's what I'm here for," Dan told her.

Grabbing the rain slicker he'd discarded when he'd let them in, Dan now followed the couple out of the clinic and locked up for a second time.

Will's truck was still parked directly in front of the clinic where he'd first left it. Cassidy hurriedly made her way over to the vehicle. But Will's stride was longer, and he beat her to it without even trying. He proceeded to open the door behind the driver's just before she reached it.

Cassidy pressed her lips together, biting back the desire to tell him that she could have opened her own door, thank you very much. Instead, she muttered a barely audible, "Thanks."

Will greeted the choked out verbal offering with a grin. His eyes were almost dancing as he asked, "Almost hurts you to say it, doesn't it?"

Cassidy got on without so much as looking at him. "Just get me to my truck," she ground out.

Rather than getting into the front seat, Will leaned over her to help her with her seat belt, just as he had the first time. But this time Cassidy was faster than he was. She grabbed the end of the belt from him.

"I can buckle my own seat belt, Laredo," she informed him.

"Just trying to make things easier for you," Will answered cheerfully.

Cassidy never skipped a beat. "That would involve disappearing off the face of the earth."

Will climbed into the cab of the truck behind the steering wheel. "Your brothers would miss you," he said.

He knew damn well what she meant. "I was referring to you."

"Maybe later," he replied glibly, and then he turned the key, starting his truck.

The next moment, they were back on the road.

The rain was starting again, Cassidy noted, but the sky didn't look nearly as foreboding as it had earlier, so she crossed her fingers and hoped for the best, praying that history didn't repeat itself. The last thing in the world she needed right now was to become stranded somewhere with the baby and with Laredo.

Neither one of them spoke for the first few minutes, with only the rain cutting into the silence. But the stillness within the truck was very short-lived.

Will was the first to break it.

"Are you sure you're up to this?" he asked.

She should have known the silence was too good to last. That she actually welcomed the break was something she would have gone to her grave before ever admitting it to him. "Was that supposed to be some kind of a crack?"

"No," Will replied mildly, his eyes all but glued on the road in front of him. He was taking no chances on driving into an unexpected sinkhole; they had been known to occur after a heavy rain. "That's just a question. I mean, quite honestly—" he raised his eyes for a second to meet hers in the rearview mirror "—I can see you wearing a hell of a lot of hats, but I *never* thought of you as the maternal type."

She frowned. It *was* a crack. Not that she had any driving need to have him think of her in any sort of a positive light, but she didn't particularly care for what she viewed as his put-down.

"Just because I have this constant, overwhelming desire to hit you over the head with a two-by-four doesn't mean I don't have any maternal instincts. I do." Her eyes narrowed as she glared at him in the mirror. "Just not any toward you."

"Which, don't get me wrong, I'm very grateful about." Had Laredo stopped there, she could have accepted it, giving it no more thought than she would have given another bad, incorrect weather forecast.

But he didn't stop there.

Will continued, saying, "I never wanted you to think of yourself as my mother."

She was having a hard time not saying what was on her mind, but she knew an explosion would have the kind of consequences she was *not* looking for—it would have set off the baby. Any moment that the baby wasn't wailing was another moment to be savored and enjoyed—even if Will was there to share it with her.

"I don't know if you accidentally meant that as a compliment," she told him, "or if it was another crack, so I'm just going to leave that alone."

She heard him laugh shortly to himself. At her expense. She was starting to suspect that just the sound of his breathing was enough to set her off.

"Good thinking," Will commented.

"Is that another accidental compliment?" Cassidy challenged.

He undoubtedly hadn't meant it that way, but she wanted to needle him, and this was her only opportunity. He owed her after having ripped through the foundations of her world with that kiss he'd laid on her earlier.

That she owed him because he had jumped into the water when he didn't have to and thus could have, very possibly, saved her life, not to mention the life of the baby who she in turn was trying to save, was beside the point and not something she wanted to dwell on at the moment.

That was something she'd reexamine some sleepless night—or maybe the reexamination of that would turn it *into* a sleepless night. She didn't really know, but in any event, she didn't want to think about either case right now.

"No, just another observation," Will replied.

He was really getting under her skin now, and while she couldn't exactly explain why, she knew she wanted him to stop doing it. Now.

"Yeah, well, I don't need you to 'observe' anything with your running commentary if you don't mind. All I want is for you to get me back to my truck so we can both go our separate ways."

"Not a good idea," he told her mildly.

Didn't the man ever just say yes and let the matter go? Cassidy wondered in exasperation.

"*What's* not a good idea?" she demanded. "Getting me back to my truck?"

"That, and you driving off on your own," he added mildly.

That really got her angry. "I drive better than you do," she retorted.

"That is a matter of opinion—although you don't," Will said. "But either way, that's not the point right now."

"And what is the point?" she asked him in a tone that could only be described as haughtily angry.

If she was trying to get him to lose his temper, she was failing miserably. He seemed determined to remain on an even keel as he spoke with her, no matter how much she poked the proverbial stick at him.

"Same thing that was the point when I drove you to the clinic," he told her, his tone mild, as if he was talking to someone who was slow-witted and had trouble following him. "You can't drive and hold on to that baby at the same time. It's not safe for either of you, although I'm more concerned about the baby than I am about you."

If he said that to get a rise out of her, she wasn't about to let that happen. Instead, she murmured, "At least you're honest."

Will nodded, again never missing a beat. "Always. I also have a point," he told her, stressing the words as he glanced up into the rearview mirror again to catch her eye. "You can't just stick the baby in the backseat and drive."

If he wasn't driving, she would have hit him. But as it was, she had to work at keeping her temper—at least for now.

"I know that. What about my truck?" she asked.

He tried to recall where she'd left it. "Barring another flash flood, it should be safe," he told her. "After you get everything set up for the baby and do whatever it is you have to do to make that happen, you can go with one of your brothers to bring it back.

"Or I could just take Connor there now after I drop you off." Except for the time he'd left Forever, he and Connor, as well as her other brothers, had been friends for as far back as he could remember. "I expect he's probably pacing around right about now, looking for something to do."

Although he was right, she didn't like what he was saying about her oldest brother. It made Connor sound like some sort of wimp.

"You were out in this," she reminded him. "The rain didn't stop you."

"I was out in this *because* of the rain," Will reminded her.

"Oh." The matter of the baby had driven the information out of her head, but she remembered now, remembered what he'd told her. "That's right, you were looking for that colt."

For just a brief moment, Cassidy's guard came down and she experienced concern for the animal's welfare. What if something had happened to the horse because he'd stopped to help her?

"I'm sorry. Do you think you'll still be able to find him after all this time?"

"I'll find him," he told her. There was no bravado in Will's voice, much as she might have wanted to accuse him of that. There was just confidence in his own abilities. "I can be stubborn if I have to be, just like you."

She raised her eyes again, expecting to meet his, but Will was once again strictly focused on the road ahead. She felt something weird for a second.

"Are we having a moment here?" she asked him.

Will wasn't able to read her tone of voice and decided that the wisest thing was just to acknowledge her words in the most general possible sense.

"I suppose that some people might see it that way," he said.

Cassidy shook her head. "Typical."

"Come again?"

Cassidy raised her voice. "I said your answer's typical. You're a man who has never committed to anything."

"Not true," Will contradicted before he could think better of it.

"Okay, name one thing," she challenged.

She was not going to box him in if that was what she was looking to do, he thought. At least, not about something that was way too personal to talk about out loud with her. Besides, he did just fine having everyone think that he was only serious about any relationship he had for a very limited amount of time. That way, if he brought about the end himself, he never had to publicly entertain the sting of failure.

"I'm committed to restoring my father's ranch, making it into the paying enterprise it should have been and still could be with enough effort," he told her.

"You mean that?"

Rather than say yes, he told her, "I never say something just to hear myself talk."

"There's some difference of opinion on that one, but—"

"Look," he began, about to tell her that he didn't want to get into yet another dispute with her over what amounted to nothing, but he never had the opportunity. The one thing that Cassidy admittedly could do better than anyone he knew was outtalk everyone.

"—if you're really serious about that," she was saying, "I can probably manage to help you out a few hours on the weekends." The way she saw it, she did owe it to him for helping her save the baby, and she hated owing anyone, most of all him.

Will spared her a glance before he went back to watching the road intently. Cassidy had managed to do the impossible.

She had rendered him completely speechless.

Chapter Seven

It took him a minute—more like two—but he finally found his voice.

"Wait, did you just actually offer to *help* me?" Will asked incredulously.

Cassidy was beginning to regret the offer already, although she knew what he had to be facing—exactly what Connor had faced when their father died suddenly, leaving them all orphaned and in debt.

"Don't sound so stunned. I didn't just say I'd marry you," Cassidy said brusquely. "I said I could give you a few hours on the weekends to help you get the ranch back on its feet. It's what neighbors do, right? They help each other. You're not the only one who can come through," she informed him. "As a matter of fact, I *have* to help you."

"And why is that?"

"Because I refuse to be in your debt."

"Oh." She was talking about his diving in to rescue her and the baby. This was her way of admitting that he'd saved her, he realized. "Okay, well, now it all makes sense," he allowed. "For a second there, I thought maybe I'd slipped into some alternate universe. You know, one where we're actually friends," he said with just a touch of sarcasm, even though he was smiling.

"Like I said," she told Will, "don't let your imagination run away with you."

His eyes met hers briefly as he thought of their moment in the clinic when who-knew-what had possessed him and he had done what he knew a lot of other men in the area all yearned to do. In his opinion, he had already gotten carried away, and once had to be more than enough. Because he might wind up being seriously doomed.

Cassidy McCullough had a body made for sin and a temperament that would make a shrew envious. That was *not* a combination that he would fare well with.

Any way he looked at it, it spelled trouble, and he intended to live a long, prosperous life. That meant avoiding, as much as humanly possible, having his path cross hers.

And yet, she was offering to help. If he turned that down, who knew what sort of consequences he would wind up reaping? Cassidy became insulted easily, and her wrath was not the sort to be taken lightly. Besides, there was no denying that he could use the help.

"Wouldn't dream of it," he told her, thinking that might call an end to the exchange.

Something in Laredo's voice challenged her, but that was for another time. Right now, there was a small human being depending on her. A small human being whose parents were probably frantically looking for him right at this very moment.

She knew she would be if she were in their shoes.

"As long as we're clear," Cassidy replied. The next moment, she leaned forward as far as she could in the backseat.

"There's the house," she said, pointing to it.

"I know what your house looks like, Cassidy," he replied. "I was just away for a few years. I wasn't strapped to some gurney, having my brain wiped clean by some evil scientist."

The latter was a reference to the superhero comic books they had all read as kids. Back then, they had pooled their money together to buy one each month as it came out, and then they'd pass it around, each taking their turn reading about whatever adventures were taking place in the current issue.

By the time she would get her turn, the pages had been folded countless times, not to mention faded. Consequently, some of the lettering was hardly legible. Being the youngest definitely had its drawbacks, she recalled.

"Eric Smith was a lot handsomer than you," she recalled, mentioning the hero he was referring to by the character's secret identity.

"He was a comic-book hero," Will reminded her. "He was drawn that way."

"I know. Makes the truth that much sadder, doesn't it?" she asked, looking at him pointedly.

He could almost feel her eyes boring into the back of his head.

The next second, he was calling her attention to something else.

"Looks like you've got a welcoming committee," Will observed, nodding at the front door. It was opening, and the next second, Connor came out.

The oldest McCullough didn't exactly look happy, Will observed.

"Where the hell have you been?" Connor demanded the moment Cassidy opened her door. Connor walked over to the truck quickly. "Why didn't you call, and why are you so wet? It's raining, but you look like you've been swimming in the river."

Reaching the truck, her brother saw the baby in her arms just as he was starting to cry. His brow furrowed. "What are you doing with Cody and Devon's baby?" he asked.

"Nothing," Cassidy answered. "Because this isn't their baby." She passed the baby to him before getting out of the truck. Once her feet were on the ground, she reclaimed Adam.

Somewhat dumbfounded, Connor turned toward Will.

"You make sense out of this for me?"

Will merely shrugged. "Hey, she's your sister. I haven't understood a thing she's said since the day I met her."

"Come in before it starts raining again," Connor ordered. The sky had darkened again, and there was every indication that it would pour despite a short, promising break in the weather.

He waited until they were all inside the house. Will brought in the supplies the doctor had given them for Adam. Closing the door behind him, Connor faced the two of them. "Now, whose baby is this?" he asked. And now that he'd gotten a closer look at Will, he must have noticed that the latter was in the same condition as his sister. "What the hell were you two doing out there, and how does it involve this baby? You *both* look like you've been swimming in the river."

"There's a reason for that," Cassidy told her brother, shifting the baby to her other arm. Adam was small, but he wasn't exactly weightless.

"I'm listening," Connor said, waiting.

She glanced at Will, thinking that he might jump in and interrupt her. When he didn't—there'd always been something about Connor that put Will on his best behavior, she thought grudgingly—Cassidy went on to answer her brother's questions.

"I saw the baby caught up in the flash flood, and I dove in to rescue him."

"I rescued her rescuing him," Will added, filling in his part in the story.

Connor's eyes went from his sister to his friend, speaking volumes even as he remained silent and continued to wait.

Connor could always make her squirm, she thought, annoyed. She shrugged. "Maybe he did at that."

"I look forward to hearing the details," Connor told them. "But right now, why don't you both change out of those wet clothes? I've got some clothes in my bedroom that'll fit you, Will."

As he spoke, Connor took the baby from his sister with the confidence of a man who had expertly taken care of his three siblings over the years, as well as, most recently, his niece. "I'll just wait for you down here with the baby. Whose is it?" he asked again as they both began to head for the staircase.

"That's the big mystery," Cassidy replied, starting to take the stairs two at a time.

"Wait, what?" Connor asked. Babies didn't just appear out of nowhere like in some fairy tale. Babies had parents and a definite entry point.

"We brought him to the clinic to get checked out," Will told him. "But the doc didn't recognize him. Couldn't tell us who he belonged to. Then I called the sheriff about it—"

"—and he's having Cody and Joe look into it," Cassidy concluded as she hurried the rest of the way up the stairs. Her clothes were starting to feel clammy as they stuck to her, and she welcomed the thought of changing into something dry and more comfortable.

"Will," Connor called to him, stopping the other man for a moment. Will turned and looked at him, waiting. "Thanks." He didn't elaborate any further.

He didn't have to.

Will shrugged away Connor's words. "Couldn't exactly let her drown, now, could I?" he asked glibly. "Wouldn't do that to my worst enemy—come to think of it…" Will's voice trailed off as he grinned.

"Right," Connor replied, knowing the game that went on between his sister and the man he and his brothers had known—and liked—all of their lives. "Just go change."

Left alone, Connor gazed down at the baby in his arms. Bright blue eyes looked back up at him, as if trying to absorb everything in the immediate area and make sense of it.

"Well, you look none the worst for the experience," Connor observed. "Want to give me a clue?" he asked. "Just whose baby are you?"

The baby just went on looking up at him.

HE WAS STILL wondering that several minutes later when both Will and his sister came back downstairs.

Cassidy, he noticed, might be trying to assume an air of complete disinterest and nonchalance, but she'd dried and combed out her hair rather than just catching it back in a wet ponytail the way she might have when they were a lot younger. And she'd put on a light blue blouse, one that brought out the color of her eyes.

She'd gone to some trouble to look good for a man she claimed not to be able to stand. He wondered how much longer she was going to continue to play that game.

"What do you plan to do about this baby?" Connor asked once they were both downstairs.

"Do?" Cassidy echoed.

"Yes, do. A baby takes a lot of work," he reminded her.

She didn't like being put on the spot, especially with Laredo witnessing all this. "I know that. I thought that we could all take turns."

"And just when would your turn come up? As I recall, you're normally putting in some pretty long hours at the law firm. Cody's got a full-time job—not to mention a wife and baby to take care of—and Devon's teaching," he reminded his sister, referring to Cody's wife. "Cole's working at The Healing Ranch now, and that leaves me running the ranch here."

Cassidy felt overwhelmed for a moment. She glanced in Will's direction, but rather than say anything about him, she asked, "What about Rita?" Connor had recently hired the young woman on what amounted to a part-time basis. She did some light cleaning, and occasionally cooked dinner since all of them had taken on more responsibilities in the last few months. "She comes from a large family. A baby should be a piece of cake for her."

"Having a large family doesn't immediately qualify her to take care of a baby," Connor pointed out. The baby was fussing, so he shifted the infant to his other arm, then began to slowly rock the child.

"Why don't we just ask her if she'd like to pitch in? Between all of us, we'll be able to handle one little baby," she told her brother with confidence. "Besides, this could all be just for a short duration, just until Adam's parents can be found."

"Adam?" Connor repeated somewhat uncertainly. "You know his name?" If that was the case, then locating the parents shouldn't be a problem.

"No," she admitted, quickly adding, "We thought it might be helpful to have something to call him while we try to find his parents and take care of him. The name was Will's idea."

Connor wasn't sure if she was giving the other man credit, or blaming him. He looked at Will. "So it's a boy?"

"You can't tell?" Will asked, feigning surprise.

Connor looked at him as if his friend was kidding. "It's a baby," he said pointedly. "At this age, they all look alike."

Will laughed, amused.

Cassidy wasn't. "If you ever get married and wind up having one of these little people yourself, make sure that your wife never hears you say that," she warned her brother.

"If I ever do get married—" something Connor highly doubted, given that his life was almost always all about work and, until not that long ago, about watching out for his siblings "—and have one of these, I'll know what it is when it's born. There'll be no reason to say that they all look alike."

"Look, why don't I just take him with me?" Will offered.

Cassidy turned to stare at him as if he'd lost his mind. "You?" she questioned, looking at Will incredulously. What did he know about taking care of a baby?

"Yeah, why not?" Will asked, taking offense at her tone. "I know I can take care of a baby as well as you can."

Connor sighed. "As entertaining as this anything-you-can-do-I-can-do-better refrain might be, why don't the two of you put aside this competition thing you've had going on since forever and join forces to take care of this little guy until we find out just what his future is going to be?"

"Join forces?" Cassidy echoed as if her brother had

suddenly lapsed into a foreign language. "You mean like, live together?"

Connor nearly choked at the very mention of the idea. "I don't think the world is ready for that kind of warfare just yet. I was thinking more along the lines of you two each pitching in a few hours a day."

"Laredo's got a ranch to run by himself, remember? He can't very well strap the baby onto his back," Cassidy protested. "I've got a better idea. I'll take the baby into work with me tomorrow."

Both Connor and Will stared at her as if now *she* was the one speaking in a foreign tongue. "What?" Cassidy challenged. "Olivia's a mother. She can appreciate the problems that arise with having a baby."

"This isn't your baby," Will pointed out.

"Doesn't matter whose he is," Cassidy insisted. "The point is that he is *a* baby, and he needs to be taken care of. She's got a couple of her own—as does Cash," she reminded them. "They'll probably be very helpful."

There were times when her optimism astonished Will, given her usual personality. No doubt about it. Cassidy McCullough was a mystery on two legs. Two very long, shapely legs.

"She's good when it comes to volunteering other people, isn't she?" Will asked her oldest brother, amused by the liberties she assumed.

"Always," Connor agreed. "But maybe you have something there," he told Cassidy. "And who knows? Maybe by then Cody or Joe will be able to find out who Adam's parents are."

"Or at least what happened to them," Will added grimly.

"You think they were lost in the flash flood?" Connor asked him.

"It is a possibility," Will acknowledged.

"That would make this little guy an orphan." Connor looked at the infant with new interest. "Maybe you came to the right place after all, little guy," he said, addressing the baby.

"Are you going to be here for a while?" Cassidy suddenly asked her brother.

"Why?"

"Because I still have to get my truck, and if you're okay with watching Adam here for a little bit, Laredo can drive me back to where I left it."

She turned toward the other man. "Right?" she asked him pointedly.

"Nothing would give me greater pleasure than to drop you off somewhere," Will answered, forcing a smile. It appeared utterly fake.

"That okay with you?" he asked Connor.

"Go, take her." One arm securely around the baby, Connor waved his sister away and toward Will with his free hand. "The sooner she gets her truck, the sooner she'll be back herself."

"You heard the man," Cassidy said to Will. "Let's go."

Will sighed, following her out the front door. "Somewhere in the world," he commented, "there is a small country missing its dictator."

Chapter Eight

Neither one of them spoke as they got into Will's truck. Nor were any words exchanged once they got back on the road. The silence seemed only to grow louder and more encompassing as they continued to travel back to the site where she had left her truck.

After a few minutes, the silence almost seemed deafening. Cassidy leaned over and turned on the radio. Despite the fact that she turned it up as far as it could go, no sound came out. Cassidy tried again, turning it off and then on again. Still nothing.

Biting back a few choice words, Cassidy tried pressing a few of the buttons, thinking that perhaps a couple of the stations were down, but, obviously, the radio itself wasn't connecting.

In response to the frustrated sigh she exhaled, Will told her, "It's dead."

"I kind of figured that out," she answered curtly. "Can't you fix it?"

The radio, like the truck itself, had had its share of problems. "Not worth fixing," he replied.

How could he stand driving around without a radio?

In her opinion, music made everything more tolerable. "Then get a new one."

He didn't even spare her a glance. "Not exactly high on my priority list right now."

There was an entire host of expenses facing him. He didn't have the money to waste on a new radio, and he wasn't handy enough to bring the car radio back from the dead.

Cassidy contemplated lapsing back into silence, but the idea was just not appealing. Even arguing with Laredo was better than riding along in this all-encompassing silence.

Desperate for some sort of noise, Cassidy decided to try her luck at getting him to talk. "You know, I didn't think you'd stick around after Cody's wedding."

"You didn't think I'd stick around, or you *hoped* I wouldn't stick around?" he asked, glancing in her direction.

They knew each other better than either of them was really willing to admit. "Both," she answered. "When my brothers told me you had that big, knock-down, drag-out fight with your father and then just rode out of town, I really thought we'd seen the last of you."

She'd almost slipped and made it more personal by saying, "I," but she'd caught herself just in time. That was all she needed, to have Laredo think that she had some sort of personal stake in his being around.

"Well, you were the one who sent that letter from Olivia's firm, notifying me about my father's will, telling me that he left the ranch to me. I wouldn't be here if you hadn't." He'd always figured that his father was too ornery to die and would go on living on the ranch forever. The letter he'd received had knocked him for a loop. It took him a while to reconcile himself to the facts. "How did you track me down, anyway?" he asked.

"I had nothing to do with it," she informed him. Then because he was looking at her, waiting for her to own up to the deed, she said, "Connor knew where to find you. And anyway, that notification wasn't from me personally. As I already mentioned, I was told to draft the letter on behalf of the law firm." Thinking he might need more of a background than that, she said, "Your father had Olivia draft the will leaving the property to you."

Will heard the words, but he still couldn't really make any sense out of what he was hearing. He shook his head. "That doesn't sound like the old man. Leaving all his debts for me to pay sounds more like him," he had to admit, "but not the ranch."

She knew what he was saying was right, but facts were facts, and Jake Laredo had indeed come into the office and dictated his will. Not a word had been changed.

"Some people have a change of heart when they know they're dying," she told him.

Will laughed shortly. For as far back as he could remember, there had never been any love lost between his father and him. For some reason, his father always blamed him for his mother leaving. It was easier that way than to blame himself.

"To have a change of heart, the old man would have had to have one," Will told her. He kept his eyes on the road, not trusting himself to look at her. He didn't want her glimpsing what he was trying to bury. "That man was as cold-blooded as they came." He paused, then added, "I never blamed my mother for running off."

"Not for running off," Cassidy agreed. "But she should have taken you with her, not left you behind."

All that had happened years ago. He'd been only seven at the time. He remembered crying himself to sleep for weeks. That was something he'd never shared with anyone. "Wanted to be rid of me even then, is that it?"

"Hey, you were always giving me a hard time," she reminded him, playing along for the moment. "But for the record, I meant that if she knew your father was such a mean-spirited son of gun, she shouldn't have left you. Your mother should have tried everything she possibly could to take you with her. Mothers have a responsibility to look after their children's welfare."

Damn, she hadn't meant to sound as if she was preaching. If he was okay with what had happened, then who was she to rail against it? She had no stake in this. But even so, she couldn't help feeling for the boy Laredo had once been, abandoned by his mother and mistreated by his father. It had been a hard fate.

Will deliberately shifted the conversation away from himself. "Think that's what Adam's mother was trying to do?" he asked. "Putting him into that pink tub to save his life?"

Cassidy didn't doubt it for a second. "It did the trick, so I guess the answer to that is yes." The alternative to that was that Adam had been abandoned, but as far as she could see, that was highly doubtful. "It's not like she—if it was his mother—had exactly planned all this. That flash flood today came out of nowhere. The forecast I heard was for rain, not sudden storms and flash floods."

She paused for a moment, then, because her conscience goaded her, she forced herself to stumble through an apology. She was totally unaccustomed to rendering one unless absolutely necessary, and while she had no problem when it came to slicing Will Laredo down to size, bringing up painful memories of his less than happy childhood was in her estimation a low blow. She hadn't meant to remind him of it.

The childhood she and her brothers had shared was by no means a happy-go-lucky one. She'd never known her mother, and she and her brothers had had to work long and hard for everything they had, but there was always love in the family. That was something she knew that Will never had in his.

It was also why, she knew, that he'd always been so drawn to her own family. While her father had been alive, he'd treated Will with respect and decency—and her brothers regarded him as one of them. They never clashed with Laredo the way she always did. But even that had come out of a sense of competition that existed between her brothers and her. In a way, she'd regarded Will as another brother herself.

"Look, I didn't mean to bring up any bad memories," she told him, trying to find the right words to convey that she'd made a mistake and for that, for dredging up any painful memories, she was sorry.

Will shrugged. "Don't worry about it," he told her in a completely dismissive tone. It irritated her, but she knew why he sounded like that. In his place, she had to admit that she would have spoken the same way. Vulnerability was not something either one of them really owned up to.

"There's your truck." He pointed to the vehicle just up ahead.

She breathed a sigh of relief. "At least it didn't wash away," she murmured.

The truck had been secondhand when she'd gotten it, but it got her to and from town, which was all that really mattered. Someday she would get a new truck. Maybe even a new sedan instead. Trucks were far more practical given the terrain, but she had to admit she found a sleek sedan very appealing.

But all that was a long way away. First she had to get her final degree and join Olivia's firm in earnest, as an associate, not just an intern.

Will pulled up right behind her truck. Cassidy lost no time in getting out.

"Thanks," she tossed over her shoulder as she went to the driver's side of her less than pristine vehicle. If anything, the rain seemed to have made it dirtier, not cleaner.

Opening the door, she was about to get in when she realized that Will hadn't pulled out the way she'd expected him to. She'd taken up almost half his day. What was he waiting for?

"Something wrong?" she asked.

He inclined his head. "That's what I'm waiting to find out."

That made no sense to her, and her expression indicated as much. "Just what is that supposed to mean?"

He put it into plain English for her. "I thought I'd wait to see if your truck started up again."

"Why shouldn't it?" she asked suspiciously. What did he know that she didn't? Had he done something to her truck before diving in to help her save Adam?

"'Cause your truck is over twelve years old, and you can never tell with these old trucks. I just don't want to have you on my conscience if you wind up being stranded out here after I leave."

Her eyes narrowed as she regarded him. "Since when did you develop a conscience?" she asked.

"I've always had one," he informed her. "You were just too busy trying to find new ways to torment me to ever notice."

"As I recall, you were the one trying to torment me."

"Cassidy…" There was a warning note in his voice.

"Yes?"

He couldn't tell if she was getting ready to go another round with him or just waiting for him to go on talking. He waved at the vehicle up ahead. "Just start the damn truck."

"Since you put it so sweetly," she said, swinging into the driver's seat.

The next moment, Cassidy put the key into the ignition and turned it. The truck seemed to sputter once, then again. On the third try, the engine finally turned over and the truck came to life.

She turned to tell him he could go home now and saw that he was already doing just that. Will was backing up his truck and then turned it around, heading, she assumed, to his own ranch.

Cassidy gunned her engine and tore out.

SHE LEFT FOR town early the next morning. Cassidy felt she had a stop to make before she went into work. She was heading for Miss Joan's.

Miss Joan's Diner was the only restaurant in Forever. It had been that way as far back as any of the local residents could remember. The woman who ran the place was not a local herself, but it seemed as if she had been running the diner for as long as there had been a diner to run. As far as the town was concerned, both were beloved fixtures.

"Want you to meet someone," Cassidy told the baby as she took him, along with the car seat she'd borrowed, out of the backseat of her vehicle.

The tall, thin, redheaded woman, who always seemed to be somewhere within the diner, was looking in her direction when Cassidy walked in.

There were times, like now, Cassidy thought, that Miss Joan's hazel eyes seemed to look into a person's very soul.

The moment she walked into the diner, Miss Joan beckoned her over to the counter. She was looking directly at the baby.

"Is that the baby you and the Laredo boy rescued?" Miss Joan asked.

There were times when the woman took her breath away. It was obvious that Miss Joan already had the answer to the question she asked, but Cassidy said, "Yes," just to be polite.

She'd gotten the car seat that Adam was in from Cody. Her brother had an extra one, thanks to the baby shower that Miss Joan had thrown for his wife. Miss Joan could always be counted on to come through in any emergency. Right now, Cassidy was hoping the woman could come through with some information, as well.

Cassidy put the baby and the car seat on the counter so that Miss Joan could get a better look at the boy.

"Looks pretty healthy for someone who'd gone through the kind of ordeal he just did." And then she raised her eyes to Cassidy's and told her, "No, I don't recognize him."

Cassidy could only stare at the older woman. This was unnerving, even for Miss Joan. "How did you know I was going to ask you that?"

"Why else would you bring him here this early? Unless you were hoping one of the girls could watch him for you," she suggested. "We're not busy right now, so if you'd like to drop him off for a few hours…"

But Cassidy shook her head. She wasn't about to impose on Miss Joan like that unless she had no other option. "No, that's very generous of you, but I just—"

"Hell, I'm not being generous, girl. Don't you know everybody likes seeing a cute baby? Customers'll stick around a little longer, eat a little more while they're here, just to look at him. Only makes good business sense to have the kid around," Miss Joan told her matter-of-factly.

Cassidy merely nodded. She knew better than to argue with the woman. She also knew that Miss Joan enjoyed playing the part of a "tough old broad," as she liked to refer to herself on occasion. But everyone in town knew that the woman had a heart of gold, and anyone in trouble could always rely on her to come through.

They also knew better than to thank Miss Joan profusely for her help. She and her brothers would forever be indebted to the woman for being their surly guardian angel in more than half a dozen different ways when their father died suddenly. Even with Connor taking over as their guardian, they were faced with some really hard times. Miss Joan always found jobs for them to do, playing the hard taskmaster. She always made sure that they were never hungry.

Cassidy had no idea how they would have been able to make it without the woman's help.

"I'll keep your offer in mind," she told Miss Joan. "But I'm going to take him with me this morning." Despite Miss Joan's statement that she didn't recognize the boy, Cassidy looked at her hopefully. "I was just hoping that maybe you recognized him so that the sheriff and Cody could try to find his mother."

Miss Joan shook her head. "Don't know who she is, but I'll have my girls ask around," she promised Cassidy. She paused to look down at the baby again. "Can't see somebody not recognizing that face once they've seen it." She leaned closer to the baby. "We'll find your mama for you, little man."

One of the waitresses approached Miss Joan, leaving a small bag, neatly folded on the top, in front of her on the counter. Miss Joan, in turn, pushed the bag toward Cassidy.

Cassidy didn't take the bag immediately. Instead, she asked, "What's that?"

"That's for you," Miss Joan replied brusquely. Her manner silently indicated, *Who else would it be for?*

"But I didn't order anything," Cassidy politely pointed out.

Miss Joan's thin eyebrows narrowed over her nose. "I didn't say you did, did I? You haven't changed a bit since you were a little girl. Always arguing. You better hope that he's not like that," Miss Joan told her, nodding at the little boy.

"Won't matter one way or another," Cassidy replied. "He's either going with his mother when we find her, or if she doesn't turn up, I guess that social services'll take him."

"Is that the same social services your big brother worked himself to the bone to keep you, Cody and Cole away from?" Miss Joan asked pointedly, already aware of the answer to that question, as well.

That was a sharp jab to her conscience, Cassidy thought. But then, Miss Joan had never been one to pull her punches.

Picking up the car seat, Cassidy reached for the paper bag that Miss Joan had had prepared for her. She made no effort to answer the rhetorical question that had been put to her.

Instead, she nodded at Miss Joan. "Thanks for the coffee and whatever else is in here," she said as she began to leave.

"Could just be your conscience," Miss Joan said, addressing the back of her head as Cassidy made her way across the diner to the front door.

The woman still knew how to deliver a well-aimed remark to skewer her, Cassidy thought as she made her way back out to the street.

"And that," she told Adam as she brought him to her truck and secured his car seat to the restraints that were built into the truck, "for future reference, is Miss Joan. Don't let her scowl scare you. Woman's got a heart of gold. You just have to mine through a lot of hard rock to get to it. But it's well worth the effort." She checked the ties to make sure they held. "Okay, next stop, reality," she quipped.

Cassidy started her truck and headed off to the law office.

Chapter Nine

"Well, I must say, the clients seem to be getting younger and younger these days," Olivia commented when she saw Cassidy walking in with Adam. Crossing to her, Olivia took a closer look at the baby. "This isn't Cody's little girl, is it? As a matter of fact, it's not a little girl at all." Olivia looked at her intern, her curiosity aroused. "Cassidy, whose little boy is this?"

For the moment, because it felt as if the baby was getting heavier by the second, Cassidy placed the car seat on the floor next to the chair in front of Olivia's desk. "That's just the problem—we don't know."

"We?" Olivia questioned.

"She means her and Will Laredo," Cash Taylor told his partner as he walked in on the exchange. Surprised, he looked at Olivia. "You mean that you haven't heard?" he asked.

"I had my hands full last night with a couple of kids who were convinced we were all going to float away at any minute—and Rick didn't get home until late, which just made things worse in their minds. When he did get home, he fell into bed, face-first. He was up and gone again before I was awake." Olivia shook her head. Being a sheriff's wife took a great deal of understanding and patience. "The storm did a lot of damage at the south end of town." Olivia looked from her partner to their intern. "Heard what?"

Cash answered before Cassidy could say anything. "We're in the presence of a hero—or at least one of them," he amended. Cash willingly filled in the details as he had heard them related by his stepgrandmother, Miss Joan.

"Seems that our intern here saw this little guy smack in the middle of what used to be the creek that runs by the Laredo place, being swept away. Miss Joan said she'd heard he was in some kind of a plastic container. Cassidy dove in to save him."

"How does Will Laredo fit into all this?" Olivia asked.

"Story is that he dove in to save Cassidy saving the baby," Cash replied.

"I would have been fine," Cassidy protested for what felt like the hundredth time. And then she shrugged. "But Laredo likes taking charge of things."

"Those kinds of things can get ugly really fast," Cash said. "Maybe it was a lucky thing that Will was there."

Cassidy couldn't bring herself to agree outright. The closest she could come was to vaguely echo the word Cash had just used.

"Maybe," she allowed. "All I know was that I had the baby and I was heading for the bank when Laredo grabbed us both from behind, so I'll never really know if I needed his help or not." She conveniently left out the part where her arms felt like lead right about that time.

In her opinion, that was enough talk about Laredo. She had something more pressing on her mind right now. Since the firm had been initially started by Olivia, she felt it only right to put the question to the woman regarding the baby. "Is it all right if I have him stay here today? I know I should have called and asked you first, but—"

Olivia nodded knowingly. "But it's better to ask for forgiveness than for permission, right?" Not waiting for an answer, Olivia crouched beside the car seat and smiled. The baby returned her smile by looking at her with wide, wide eyes. "I think we can set something up to keep this little guy happy and out of the way." For a moment, Olivia watched as the baby seemed content to play with his toes. Rising to her feet, she commented wistfully, "This really takes me back."

"Thinking of having another one?" Cash asked her, amused.

"Thinking of borrowing one on occasion, maybe," Olivia corrected her partner. "I've had my share of diapers and staying up all night just to come into the office the next morning so groggy and beat that I could hardly sit up in my chair."

Cassidy thought of last night. She'd kept the baby in her room, not wanting to disturb Connor or Cole, but as it turned out, she needn't have worried.

"I guess that Adam must be ahead of the game because for the most part, he slept all through the night."

"Adam?" Olivia questioned.

"The baby," Cassidy explained, realizing that she hadn't used the name before.

"How do you know his name?" Olivia asked.

"I don't," Cassidy confessed. "But we felt we had to call him something until we could find his family, and 'Adam' seemed like the logical choice." She paused and then felt somewhat obligated to add, "It was Laredo's choice."

"Adam," Cash repeated in his resonant voice. The baby stopped playing with his toes and looked in the lawyer's direction. "How about that? He seems to respond to the name." Cash grinned at her. "You and Will might be on to something."

Not wanting to be lumped together with Laredo, Cassidy changed the subject. "It might have partially been my fault that your husband didn't get home until late last night," she told Olivia.

"Your fault?" Olivia repeated. Amusement curled the corners of her mouth. Enrique Santiago was as honorable a man as she had ever met, and she trusted him implicitly. She wasn't one of those women who jumped to conclusions even under the worst of conditions—and this was not one of those occasions, even though her intern had worded her sentence rather badly. "Why's that?"

"I reported where we first saw Adam, thinking that maybe his parents might be around there somewhere, looking for him," she stated.

Olivia nodded, filling in the missing pieces. "Knowing Rick, he probably went to check it out and scoured the area himself." She shook her head, a fond expression slipping over her face. "My husband delegates but also can't help getting involved. He takes a lot of pride in saying that this is his town, and he can take care of whatever needs doing."

Olivia went around to the other side of her desk and took her seat. "Since he didn't get in touch with you, my guess is that he couldn't find any sign of the baby's parents or their car."

"Maybe there was no car," Cash suggested, turning the thought over in his mind.

"Adam's too little to have walked to the creek," Cassidy pointed out. "According to Dr. Dan, he's maybe three months old."

"But it wasn't a creek yesterday, was it?" Olivia said, picking up on what her partner was driving at.

"No," Cassidy agreed. "Yesterday it was more like a river," she recalled. She tried not to think about it. It had all been rather frightening how quickly everything had evolved.

"How far back did the 'river' go?" Cash asked her. "Did you happen to notice?"

Cassidy shook her head. "All I noticed was the baby. I was about to take shelter in that old run-down cabin on Laredo's property when I heard Adam crying. Once I realized it wasn't my imagination—that I was actually hearing a baby—I really didn't take any notice of anything else," Cassidy confessed.

"Consciously," Olivia stressed. When Cassidy looked at her curiously, the woman went on to say, "But we notice more things than we realize."

"What are you getting at?"

"I think that this little guy just might be from around here after all," Olivia suggested. She exchanged glances with Cash. "You go out far enough from town, you wind up at the reservation."

"You think that this is a Navajo baby?" Cash asked.

"I think that it's possible he might be from around that area." She looked at Cassidy. "Why don't you go talk to Joe Lone Wolf?" she suggested, mentioning her husband's senior deputy.

She thought of checking in with the sheriff later, during her lunch break. This was hardly past breakfast. "But I have work to catch up on," Cassidy protested.

Olivia smiled. "Honey, it's not that I don't appreciate your dedication, but we're a small firm in a small town. There's nothing here that can't wait for a few days if it has to. But his mother might be beside herself if she has to wait that extra time," she pointed out.

"As long as it's all right with you," Cassidy said, picking up the baby and his car seat from the floor.

"It's my suggestion. Of course it's all right with me." She waved Cassidy out of her office. "Just let me know what happens," she called out after Cassidy.

"Absolutely," the younger woman promised.

Cash went out in front of her to hold open the door as she carried Adam out in the car seat. "Thank you," she told him as she passed by.

Cassidy could feel her arms aching in protest as she went back to her vehicle. "I am going to have really large biceps by the time we find your mama," she told the baby. Opening the door to the truck's rear seat, she felt as if she'd only taken the restraining straps off the baby seat a minute ago, and here she was, putting the straps back around the car seat as she got Adam situated again. "I guess that comes in handy when you're working on a ranch, but it doesn't look all that attractive for a legal intern working at a law firm."

Adam gurgled, as if he was making a response to her observation. Bubbles cascaded from his tiny lips, making Cassidy laugh. She closed the rear door and then got in behind the steering wheel.

"I'll take that as a compliment," she told the baby cheerfully.

It took Cassidy next to no time to arrive at the sheriff's office. The latter was located several streets down from the law firm.

After getting out of the vehicle again, she went through the tedious process of removing the restraining straps and then taking the baby and the car seat out for the second time in half an hour. She thought of her sister-in-law and wondered how Devon could put up with having to do that over and over again without going crazy.

Some women were cut out for motherhood, but she didn't think she numbered among them.

Cassidy used her back to push open the front door to the sheriff's office, which was why she didn't see him immediately. But once she and the baby were inside, she not only saw the bane of her existence, she heard him, as well. The sound of his deep voice cut straight to the bone.

On any other day, she might have just turned and walked right out, but this wasn't any other day. And besides, this wasn't about her. This was about the baby.

A baby who needed answers more than she needed to avoid Will Laredo.

"What are you doing here?" she demanded the moment she crossed the threshold and noticed Will talking to both her brother Cody, as well as Joe Lone Wolf. From the looks of it, the sheriff wasn't around.

"Last I checked, this was a public office," Will replied. "And not that I need to answer your questions, but I came in to find out if any progress was being made in locating Adam's mother or father."

"I just saw Cody last night," she reminded Will, waving a hand impatiently in her brother's general direction. "If any headway had been made, I would have known about it."

"Yes, but you're not exactly inclined to share that kind of information with me, are you?" Will asked. "And since I'm involved here, I have an equal right to know, same as you."

Joe frowned as he looked at the squabbling duo. "You two keep going at it, you're going to make this kid cry, not to mention me," he told them in his low, calm voice.

He nodded toward Will and said, "Will here thinks that maybe the baby might be from the reservation."

Cassidy made no comment about Will's thinking one way or another. She certainly didn't like sounding as if they were on the same side, but she had to ask, "Is he?"

"If you're asking me if I recognize him, I don't," Joe said. "But I haven't been up around the reservation for months, so I really couldn't say for sure. What I am willing to do is go up there and ask around." He looked at the baby and just the barest hint of a smile crossed his lips. "Might not be a bad idea to take this little guy with me, see if anyone recognizes him. So whenever you two feel like calling a truce, I'm ready to go with you and your foundling to the reservation."

Cody laughed as he shook his head. "If you're waiting for them to call a truce, the kid'll be ready for college by that time. Maybe even older."

Cassidy gave her brother a dirty look. "You're supposed to be on my side."

"There aren't supposed to *be* any sides," her brother informed them matter-of-factly. "The only thing that's supposed to matter here is finding this baby's parents— or at least one of them," he reminded the couple he was looking at.

"He's right, you know," Will said to her.

Cassidy found it rather difficult to be agreeable or even docile when she could feel her back going up because of something Will was saying to her. "So now you're lecturing me?"

"No, what I'm trying to do is bring about that truce," Will told her.

Right, she thought, like he thought he was going to accomplish that by talking down to her in front of the others.

"You've got a funny way of showing it," she informed him coldly.

Will bit back a few well-chosen words. Getting into it with her wasn't going to do any of them any good, and he was tired of squabbling with Cassidy. Besides, they were wasting time.

"Why don't I just start over again and say I'm sorry?" he said.

The offer caught her off guard. She just stared at him. Exactly what was he up to? "Sorry about what?"

"Sorry that I keep setting you off all the time. Look, we can pick this up later if you want," Will said. "But right now, since Joe's free, why don't we take him up on his offer and bring Adam up to the reservation? Who knows? Maybe we'll finally get some answers about who he is and what happened."

In Cassidy's eyes, agreeing with Will was like capitulating. She turned toward Joe. "I'm ready to go anytime you are."

"Hallelujah," she heard Will murmur behind her.

Chapter Ten

All four of them rode to the reservation in Joe's all-terrain vehicle. He felt it kept things simple—having two to three vehicles arrive on the reservation at the same time would call undue attention to them and definitely put the local residents on their guard.

Because he was a representative of the law in the area, there were those on the reservation who viewed Joe as an outsider despite the fact that he had grown up there. They felt he had turned his back on his people. Those were the ones who refused to accept any help from anyone who lived outside the reservation's borders.

However, not everyone thought that way, and conditions on the reservation were improving. Not fast enough in Joe's opinion, but at least they were better now than they had been when he was growing up there. Homes were no longer in disrepair, and the reservation school had been built up over the last decade, going from a small, old-fashioned single room facility to one where all the grades, from the first to the twelfth year, were now being taught.

Just recently a kindergarten had been opened, along

with a small day care so that working mothers who were employed both on and off the reservation had somewhere to leave their children while they worked.

"It looks better than the last time I was here," Will commented as he looked around.

"It has taken a lot to improve things here," Joe said honestly. "Efforts to help the locals aren't always welcomed with open arms. Some see an extended hand as a handout and take it as an insult."

"Can't you say anything to change their minds?" Cassidy asked. To her, Joe represented a success story, as did the two brothers who ran The Healing Ranch, a ranch that used horses as a way to get through to troubled teens.

"Not easily," Joe said quietly. "A lot of people on the reservation think I've sold out."

In those people's opinions, there was no such thing as being able to walk in both worlds. It had to be either one or the other, and since he was a deputy sheriff, that meant that Joe had made his choice and turned his back on his heritage.

Cassidy was surprised to hear the deputy admit to that. She knew him to be a decent, hardworking man who was always ready to lend a hand, but he was also very private and closemouthed when it came to his personal life. To have him say that some of the same people he'd grown up with now took a dim view of him was surprising.

She also knew it had to hurt.

"Do these people even *know* you?" she asked incredulously, becoming indignant on Joe's behalf. It really didn't take much to arouse the crusader within Cassidy.

"Apparently not," Will commented.

"They're not all like that," Joe told them, and then was forced to admit, "But enough of them are."

Joe pulled up in front of a small, single-story wooden building that, although relatively new-looking, seemed to have come out of a bygone era, one that clearly belonged in the middle of the last century. The building was what passed for a general store on the reservation.

Joe got out, explaining, "I thought I'd ask Smoky if he's heard anything about a missing baby."

"Smoky?" Cassidy repeated uncertainly. It seemed to her like an odd name for someone who lived on the reservation.

"It's obviously not his real name," Joe told her. "But he likes it. To tell the truth, I don't remember what his real name actually is. As far back as I can remember, everyone always called him Smoky."

Getting out, Cassidy rounded the back end of the vehicle in order to get Adam out of his car seat more easily. But by the time she got to the other passenger door, Will had beaten her to it and had already taken out the baby.

Cassidy stopped short. Her eyes swept over the rancher and child. Although she wanted to find some kind of fault with what Will was doing, she couldn't. "You don't look awkward holding Adam," she told him grudgingly.

He was accustomed to hearing nothing but criticism coming out of her mouth. Her compliment threw him off balance. Recovering, he responded, "You say that like it's a bad thing."

"No," she was forced to admit, "it's just that most bachelors hold babies as if they were holding a sack full of rattlesnakes."

Will's eyes crinkled at the corners. "Maybe being around you has taught me to be unafraid around everything else."

Cassidy didn't take that as a compliment. "Give me Adam," she ordered.

"Don't worry, kid," he told the baby, "she doesn't bite. Usually," he added as he handed Adam over to Cassidy.

"I take it the truce is over," Joe observed.

"It never fully went into effect," Will answered. "Cassidy can't bring herself to be civilized around me for more than a couple of minutes at a time—and even that's hard for her."

"That's because I can ignore you for only a couple of minutes at a time," Cassidy countered.

Joe gave her a long, penetrating look. "Well, for the sake of the kid, you two might want to consider giving it another shot while we're inside the general store talking to Smoky."

Will offered her a wide grin. "You heard the man, 'Sweetness,'" he said, placing one hand to the small of Cassidy's back as he ushered her and the baby into the general store.

Cassidy stiffened. Because she was holding the baby, she was forced to go along with Will's behavior. But it didn't keep her from fervently wishing she could elbow him in the ribs just once.

The man stacking a new inventory of wax beans glanced up when he heard the front door opening.

Recognition brought with it a welcoming smile, but Cassidy thought he looked a little wary, as well. "Hey, Joe, what brings you here?" Putting down the can he was about to arrange, Smoky wiped his hands on the apron tied around his waist and came forward. "Haven't seen you in a long time. Crime waves keeping you busy?" he asked with a dry laugh.

The man everyone called Smoky was shorter than Joe by a few inches. He was also heavier than the deputy by a good twenty pounds or so. His face appeared to be somewhat weathered, but taking a closer look at him, Cassidy guessed that Joe and the general-store clerk were probably around the same age.

"Same old stuff," Joe replied noncommittally. "How's your mother?" he asked politely.

"Still complaining because I'm not married," Smoky answered with a good-natured shrug. Midnight-black eyes swept over the two people and the infant beside Joe. "Bringing your friends around on a tour of the rez?" he asked.

Cassidy was about to tell the man why they were there when she felt Will's hand, which was still up against her back, press against her spine lightly. He was signaling for her to remain silent.

Ordinarily that would have the complete opposite effect, but they weren't on their own territory right now. Though it had always been there, the reservation was considered to be a different world, and, as such, she and Will were there as visitors. It was up to Joe to conduct the conversation, so, hard as it was for her, Cassidy bit her tongue and kept quiet.

"Actually," Joe told the shopkeeper, "we're here to ask if you heard anything about a baby going missing from the reservation."

It wasn't difficult to put two and two together. "Your question have anything to do this little guy?" Smoky asked, nodding at the baby that Cassidy was holding.

"Yeah." Joe kept his eyes on the other man's face. "You recognize him?"

Smoky returned the deputy's gaze. "Nope. Afraid I can't say that I do. I could ask around if you want," he offered.

Joe nodded. "I'd appreciate it."

"So what's the kid's story?" Smoky asked, apparently curious—or at least he seemed to feel the need to appear to be.

"He was found him in the creek yesterday—it had swollen up to a river by then," Joe said, still closely studying his childhood friend for some sort of indication that he recognized the baby—or knew more than he was saying.

"Swimming?" Smoky asked mildly.

The man couldn't be serious, Cassidy thought. She just couldn't keep quiet any longer. The words all but burst out of her mouth. "No, floating. Someone had put him in a pink tub."

Rather than act surprised, Smoky seemed interested and asked, "Where?"

"Halfway between town and the reservation," Will answered.

Smoky gave no indication that the story rang any bells for him.

"Like I said, I'll ask around." Just then, someone else walked into the general store. "I've got a customer," he told Joe. It was meant to signal the end of the conversation between them.

Taking out the card that the sheriff had printed for all of them, Joe placed it on the counter before the shopkeeper and tapped the bottom of the card. "That's my number if you find out anything."

Cassidy saw the storekeeper pick up the card and absently tuck it into his back pocket. She had her doubts about the card's fate.

The next minute, she felt Will's hand at her back again, this time he indicated that he was ushering her out. Although it annoyed her that he felt she needed clues in order to know what to do, she didn't want to cause any sort of a scene. She did her best to hold her tongue as she allowed herself to be guided out.

Her silence lasted only for so long.

"I know how to go in and out of a store," she informed Will between gritted teeth.

"Yes," he agreed amicably, "but you usually don't know *when*," he pointed out. Once outside, Will turned toward the deputy. "You want to ask around anywhere else, or is that it?"

"One more stop," Joe answered. "I thought we could stop by the church and see if Father Tom knows anything about this baby. He doesn't pick sides," Joe added as he drove them to the church.

Father Tom was a slight man, standing about five-seven or so. He'd run the church and ministered to those who chose to attend for close to fifteen years now. Unlike the shopkeeper, there was no wary expression in the priest's eyes when he saw Joe and the others entering the church.

Approaching Joe quickly, Father Tom embraced the deputy before extending a hearty greeting to the two strangers Joe had brought with him.

And then the priest smiled warmly at the baby in Cassidy's arms.

"Is this yours?" Father Tom asked the deputy.

"No, my two are home," Joe told the man who was the sole reason for his conversion as a young man. "We were hoping that you might recognize him." He nodded at the baby.

But the priest shook his head, looking somewhat chagrined. "Unless they happen to have a distinct look that sets them apart, until they begin to take on personalities, I'm afraid that all babies look rather alike to me. Was this one abandoned?" he asked sympathetically.

The word *abandoned* raised red flags for Will. "What makes you ask that?" he asked.

The explanation seemed relatively simple to Father Tom. "Well, it's obvious that you don't know who the parents are. Why else would you bring him here, asking if I recognized him?"

Cassidy was studying the priest as he spoke, and while he didn't sound as if he was closed off the way the shopkeeper had been, she had a feeling that there was something that the priest wasn't saying. Or maybe he felt he wasn't at liberty to say.

"Good guess, Father," Cassidy told the priest. "So no one came seeking forgiveness for having given in to temptation and now had no idea what to do with the end result of that moment of weakness?"

"No matter how general the terms are, if you're asking me about someone's confession, you know I can't say anything one way or another," the priest told her good-naturedly.

"Even if it means reuniting this baby with his mother?" Cassidy pressed.

"You're assuming the mother's from the reservation," he replied, still carefully navigating the line between admission and denial.

"Guessing, not assuming," Will interjected, correcting the priest.

"All I can do is ask around," Father Tom said as he escorted them to the small church's entrance. He held the door open as they left.

"Well, that went well," Cassidy said with a sigh as they made their way back to Joe's all-terrain vehicle.

Joe shrugged. "I didn't really expect anyone to jump up and down, waving their hand or pointing someone out for us."

Then what was the point of coming? Cassidy wanted to ask. But because she liked Joe and he was helping them, she tempered her question to sound a bit more sedate. "Then why did we come here?" Cassidy asked him.

"We came," Joe replied quite frankly, "to plant the seeds."

"Seeds?" Cassidy repeated, looking at the deputy and waiting for more details.

"Sometimes it takes a lot of patience to get someone to step forward with any information around here," Joe informed them matter-of-factly. There was no judgment in his voice. That was just the way things were around here. They had very little, so they guarded what they did have—their secrets. "People like to play things close to the vest. If this baby does belong to someone on the reservation, I wanted the word to get out that we have him and that the baby is perfectly well."

"Maybe that's all they wanted," Will pointed out, "to be reassured that the baby's all right. Now that they know that, they can just go on with their lives without saying anything or claiming him."

"Maybe," Cassidy allowed, surprising the two men she was with, especially Will. "And maybe, after a while, that won't be enough."

"What do you mean?" Joe asked.

Will knew what she was saying. "Maybe now that she knows we have the baby, the baby's mother will have second thoughts and want to reclaim him."

"That's a possibility," Joe agreed. "Another possibility is that now that his mother knows that her son is safe and with some people who risked their lives in order to rescue him, she's found the right parents for her baby."

"Right parents?" Cassidy almost choked on the term. "You mean us?" she cried, startled. She barely spared Will a glance before protesting the scenario that Joe had just come up with. "Wait a minute, there are no 'parents' in the wings here. There's just me and there's just Will. In no known universe does that translate into the right 'parents' for this baby." She was barely able to keep her voice down.

Will laughed shortly. "Don't hold back, Cassidy. Tell us what you really think."

"What I think is that this was just a waste of time," she informed the two men. "Even if the priest acted like he was holding something back, nobody is going to come forward and suddenly cry, 'That's my baby, please give him to me.'"

She deliberately scanned the area, taking note of every woman who had even momentarily turned in their direction. What she saw was mild curiosity, if that. What she didn't see was any expression of longing, secret or otherwise.

Adam's mother wasn't here.

"So what's next?" Will asked.

"That's easy. Next we go back into town so I can change Adam's diaper before someone comes along and decides to cite us for polluting the air," Cassidy quipped.

She was about to shift the baby to her other side so that she could open the vehicle's rear door and get in when Will reached around her and opened it for her. She slanted a glance at him, then muttered a perfunctory, but less than enthusiastic, "Thank you."

She could hear the smile in Will's voice as he replied, "You're welcome."

Cassidy didn't bother to look at her childhood adversary. The next moment, she more than had her hands full. Adam had decided that he had been quiet long enough. Filling his small lungs full of air, he let loose with a loud wail, making his displeasure heard by everyone within what had to be a half-mile radius.

Chapter Eleven

Olivia was hanging up her landline when she saw her intern returning. Since Cassidy still had the baby with her, Olivia came to the logical conclusion, secretly hoping she was wrong.

"No luck?"

Cassidy had intended to go straight to the cubbyhole she usually occupied when not working in Olivia's office, but since the latter had called out to her, she stopped and stepped into the woman's office. She really wished that she had better news.

"No, no luck," she confirmed. There was no point in hiding her disappointment. "I thought for sure we'd find at least his mother on the reservation." The more she had thought about it, the more it seemed to have made sense to her.

"Well, maybe he's not from the reservation," Olivia suggested. After all, it wasn't as if they had any proof. At best, it was just one possible assumption.

"I've just got this gut feeling that Adam's connected to the reservation in one way or another."

"Well, the truth has a way of coming out if you give

it enough time, so if one of his parents *is* from there," she said, nodding at the baby in Cassidy's arms, "we'll find out eventually."

"Hopefully sooner than later," Cassidy added. She looked down at the baby. Adam was scrunching up his face again, which she had already learned could only mean one thing. She wasn't certain just how much one diaper could hold. "Right now, I've got to change Adam's diaper before it gets toxic."

Olivia laughed, waving Cassidy on her way. "Good idea," she agreed. "Meanwhile, you've given me something to think about."

By now, the aroma from Adam's diaper was definitely competing with the oxygen in the room, but Cassidy couldn't bring herself to just walk away with that open-ended comment hanging in the air.

"What have I given you to think about?" she asked.

"Getting an investigator," Olivia said bluntly. "Up until now, I didn't think our firm really needed one, but now, with this coming up, I'm beginning to think it might be a good idea to have an investigator working for the firm, or at least having one on retainer. We need someone who could look into things for us, make sure all the details are straight if we have any concerns to the contrary. Or, in this case, someone who could find out if this baby's parents can be located."

Yes, Olivia nodded to herself as Cassidy hurried off to the ladies' room with Adam, hiring an investigator was definitely something to think about.

CASSIDY WAS DETERMINED to put in as long a day as she could to make up for the time she'd missed. Olivia, however, was equally determined that she leave early with the baby. Cassidy made a counteroffer, insisting on taking at least some of the work home with her so she wouldn't fall any more behind than she already was.

It was all part of not just the learning process at the law firm, but part of making her feel useful.

In the end, it was a draw. Cassidy left earlier than she'd intended, but she did leave with a satchel full of papers to work on during those snatches of time when Adam didn't need her.

When she finally arrived home, Cassidy still felt as if she'd put in a day and a half at the office even though that was far from the case.

"How do mothers do it?" Cassidy asked her small passenger as she undid his car seat from its restraints in the backseat. "I feel like I'm ready to crawl into that crib Cody lent us for you, and it's not even six o'clock yet. Must be some vitamin supplement I don't know about."

In response, Adam whimpered. He seemed ready to launch into another crying jag, but then apparently changed his mind. And just like that, the baby began to play with his toes again, which had become his newest form of fascination.

"Lucky thing I can't misplace those," Cassidy commented. "Hope you keep on playing with them until we can locate your mama."

That that might never happen was an idea she didn't want to even remotely begin to entertain—even though part of her had to admit it was a viable possibility. Although not a regular occurrence, flash floods did happen near and around Forever. Thinking about it now,

Cassidy could remember hearing about at least five flash floods during her lifetime. However, she could only recall hearing about one fatality in all those instances. Since those odds were in her—and Adam's—favor, she fervently hoped that they would continue to hold.

Busy trying to carry the baby as well as bring in her satchel, Cassidy took no notice of the truck that was parked off to the side of the house. At least not until she walked into the house.

Before she could call out to Connor to announce that she and Adam were home, Cassidy stopped dead. There was someone else standing in the living room. He had his back to the front door, and he was thumbing through the album that Connor kept on the secondhand coffee table their father had brought home one year.

Cassidy's breath caught in her throat. She knew that back anywhere.

"What are you doing here, Laredo?" she asked. Wasn't seeing him once today enough? she silently demanded in frustration. "And where's my brother?"

"Which brother?" Will asked as he turned around to look at her. "And to answer your first question, I'm waiting for you."

"Connor," she clarified. And then Cassidy replayed what Laredo had just said to her. She interpreted his response in her own way. A bolt of excitement zipped right through her as her eyes widened hopefully. "You found his mother!"

For possibly the umpteenth time since their very first clash of wills, he wondered why Cassidy McCullough had to be so damn pretty. Why didn't she have a face that made men embrace celibacy instead of nurturing thoughts where purity had no place?

Snapping out of his momentary flight of fancy, Will had to think for a moment in order to remember her question. "No," he answered, "why would you think that?"

"Because you said you were waiting for me, and I just thought—" Why was she even bothering to explain herself to this man? She didn't owe him an explanation. "If you're not waiting here to tell me that you've found Adam's mother, then why are you here?" she asked, running out of patience.

Damn him, Cassidy thought. Laredo could make her temper flare faster than any man alive.

In response, Will calmly smiled at her, which only irritated her further—and she knew that he knew it, but that still didn't change things. "I'm waiting here for you to get back with the baby because I'm here to help out."

Cassidy stared at him. What was he talking about? "Help out with what?"

Cassidy was a great many things, Will thought, most of them irritating. But he had never known her to be thickheaded before. Why was she pretending to be that way now?

Blowing out a breath, Will spelled it out for her. "Help out with the baby."

If anyone else had just said that, she would have immediately, not to mention happily, turned over the baby to them and sank down on the sofa with a huge sigh of relief. But this was Will, and although she couldn't really explain it, it went against her grain to admit to him that she needed his help—or any kind of help for that matter.

"I never said I needed help with the baby," she informed him coldly.

"You didn't have to," Will told her. Looking down at the baby, he smiled warmly at Adam. "Everyone needs help with a new baby."

"He's not a new baby," she said defensively. "Dr. Dan said he was around two or three months old."

"Let me rephrase that," Will said patiently, starting over again. "New to *you.* All babies represent a lot of work, and you're not used to taking care of one."

"Oh, but you are," she retorted sarcastically.

"The man is offering to help, Cass," Connor said in his eternally patient tone as he walked in from the kitchen. "Let him help." Connor was carrying a couple of bottles of beer. He offered one to Will.

Still holding the baby, Cassidy turned her entire body so that it blocked Will from having access to Adam. "I am *not* turning Adam over to a drunkard," she informed her oldest brother.

"He hasn't had anything to drink yet," Connor pointed out. "I just took the caps off the first two bottles. And since when did you become a teetotaler?" her brother asked. Cassidy liked sharing a beer as much as the rest of them.

"Since I brought a baby into the house," she replied, then her eyes shifted toward Will. "You can take the beer and go."

Instead, Will accepted the bottle from Connor and

then put it on the coffee table. The indication was that he could have the drink later if that was her objection.

"I'm here to pitch in," Will told her firmly. "I helped rescue him. I want to help take care of him as well—until we locate his parents."

Cassidy drew in her breath.

"You're under no obligation—" she began.

"That," Will said, cutting her short, "is a matter of opinion. I'm not here to argue with you."

"Well, you certainly could have fooled me," Cassidy retorted.

Will went on talking as if she hadn't interrupted him. "I'm here to do my fair share."

Just what was Laredo's game? Cassidy was certain he had something up his sleeve, but what? While she couldn't pinpoint what it was, she knew it had to be something that was meant to get under her skin—just like everything else he said or did.

"Duly noted," she told him crisply. "I'll tell everyone that you're a real prince." Her hands were full, so she couldn't wave him off. All she could do was say, "You're free to go."

"Cassidy," Connor interjected wearily. Will had been gone from the area for nearly four years, but it was as if nothing had changed in that time. The two still butted heads whenever they were in the same area—with his sister the bigger offender.

Cassidy shot her older brother an impatient look. "What?" Her temper was growing increasingly shorter, and she found she had to exert effort not to growl out the word.

"Shut up," Connor said in the same mild-mannered voice he might have used to describe this morning's breakfast.

Stunned, Cassidy could only stare at her brother. "What?"

"You heard me. I love you to pieces, Cassidy, but you could make a saint lose his temper. Now accept Will's help and stop arguing over the matter."

"Look, Cassidy," Will began, giving it another try. "I didn't come here to cause you any problems, I honestly came here to help. Now for once in your life, will you stop arguing with me and just let me help." It wasn't a request.

In what Cassidy later viewed as a weak moment, she refused to give in, quipping, "But arguing is half the fun."

Will gave her a look she could only interpret as a promise of things to come. Why she felt a strong pull within her very core, she couldn't begin to explain—nor did she really even want to think about it.

"We can have fun later," Will told her. "Right now, I want to help out with the baby. You can go on arguing with me all you want, but I think you should know that I'm not planning on going anywhere tonight. It's only right and fair that I help out with Adam, and I intend to do just that," he concluded, standing his ground.

"I'd listen to the man if I were you," Connor counseled.

Cassidy frowned. She was outnumbered and outmaneuvered—and she knew it. But she had never given up easily. "I really hate to set a precedent—"

"Cassidy," Connor said in a warning voice.

"—but I obviously have to, so okay, sure, give me a hand with him." With that she held Adam out to Will.

Taking the baby from her, Will couldn't help but take a whiff of the less than pleasing aroma that was part of the baby. "He needs to have his diaper changed," he told Cassidy.

The corners of her mouth curved with pleasure. "Good call."

Instead of asking her, Will looked at her brother. "How often does this happen a day?" he asked, unconsciously wrinkling his nose.

"More times than you'd care to think about," Connor answered. "C'mon." He put his hand on Will's shoulder. "I'll walk you through it."

But to his surprise, Cassidy put up her hand to stop her brother. "That's okay, let me," she said.

"You're going to change him?" Connor asked, surprised.

"If you're referring to Laredo, that's not possible," she told her brother.

He gave her a long-suffering look. "I was talking about the baby."

"Nope, not going to change him, either. But I'll gladly walk Laredo through it," she said with a wide grin.

"Why do I suddenly get the feeling that I've just walked into a trap?" Will asked as he followed Cassidy out of the room.

"I have no idea why you think or feel anything,"

she replied. "Now let's get this over with before Adam winds up getting a rash."

Connor could only shake his head as he watched his sister and his lifelong friend walk out of the room. He dearly loved Cassidy, but he'd be the first to admit there were times that she could try God's patience. He had no idea why Will was putting up with her drill-sergeant temperament. Unlike the rest of them, Will certainly didn't need to. There were no family ties to bind him to her.

As far as Connor could see, there was only one reason in the world why the two fought the way they did and why Will didn't give Cassidy a biting, formal dressing-down once and for all before he finally walked out on her—permanently.

Connor smiled to himself as he contemplated that reason now.

He'd always wanted another brother, he thought as he turned and walked back into the kitchen.

It was time to see about getting dinner on the table. The idea of hiring Rita to cook meals on a more permanent basis was beginning to sound better and better. He had to admit that they had all gotten rather spoiled with all the meals that Devon had made for them when she had first arrived.

CASSIDY STOOD TO one side of the bed, her arms folded before her chest as she watched Laredo change Adam's diaper. It was rather full, and the baby required a great deal of cleaning.

When Cassidy didn't offer a running commentary

on what he was doing or make any critical wisecracks on his method, Will glanced up at her.

This wasn't like her at all.

"Why aren't you saying anything?" he asked.

She sighed, giving him his due. He hadn't turned green when he first opened the diaper, and he hadn't surrendered, telling her she could finish up. He'd grimly done what needed to be done.

"Okay," Cassidy said. "Not bad."

"What?"

"If you're waiting for me to burst into applause, you've got the wrong person."

He didn't understand half the things that Cassidy said. "What are you talking about?"

Was he even *in* the same conversation as she was? "You just asked why I wasn't saying anything, so I said something."

"What I meant was that I'm not used to you being so quiet. I was sure that you were going to tell me what a bad job I was doing."

"I wanted to," Cassidy freely admitted, then added, "but there's only one problem."

Okay, here it came. Will had thought that since he volunteered to help out, it would have some kind of an effect on her, making her a little more easygoing and less scissor-tongued. He should have known better.

He braced himself. "And that is—"

This was hard for her, but not saying it would be too close to lying, so she made the best of it and forced out the words.

"You did a better job than I thought you would. Not

perfect," Cassidy said, quickly qualifying her statement. "But better."

Finished cleaning up and putting a fresh diaper on Adam, he nodded at Cassidy. "That sounds more like you—all except for the semi-compliment."

"Yeah, well, don't let it go to your head," she warned. "Although, I guess there's no harm in that. It'll die of loneliness up there."

Will couldn't help laughing. "Now that *really* sounds more like you."

Since Will was apparently finished, she picked up the baby from the bed. Holding Adam against her, she automatically patted the baby's bottom, a gesture that soothed both her and the baby.

"Okay," she told Will, "you changed a diaper. Now go home."

She wasn't going to get rid of him that easily. "I said I was going to help and I meant it, Cassidy," he informed her. "So I'm staying."

"Oh, joy."

She'd turned her back on Will and walked out, so he had no way of seeing that there was a smile on her face as she left the bedroom.

Chapter Twelve

The knock on the door didn't wake him up—Will had never believed in sleeping in, no matter what time he'd finally gone to bed the night before. Sleeping in was for people who had no life, no responsibilities to meet. But the knock did catch him off guard.

He was just about to go outside to begin working with the horses. He was still trying to settle in after being gone for so long, and settling in was a slow, tedious process. All his time, spare or otherwise, was devoted to trying to make a go of a ranch that had very little going for it.

Even when he was growing up here, Will remembered times always being tough, remembered his father being drunk half the time even though—or maybe because—bills kept piling up. Despite the wolf being at the door countless times, and his father's habit of losing himself in the bottom of a bottle, somehow they managed to make it from one month to the next, usually just one jump ahead of complete ruin. Sometimes it was even less than that.

Part of Will felt that he should just sell the ranch for

whatever he could get, use the money to pay off what he could and then just walk away from this part of his life.

The other part of him was determined to dig in and make a go of it, refusing to go under. Refusing to make his father's prophecy regarding his own life come true.

In essence, the ranch represented a challenge to him—a far more serious one than Cassidy did.

If this was a bill collector at the door, Will thought, approaching it, they were going to be disappointed. He wouldn't be able to make a payment until the first of the month—if then. It was the first of the year, actually. This was December, the month of miracles and, appropriately enough, Christmas. Heaven knew he could do with a miracle or two.

It was awfully warm for December, he couldn't help thinking. Recently the days had felt more like June. That was probably the main reason why he hadn't lost the colt that day of the flash flood. The horse had managed to survive until he had finally found him.

Will didn't bother asking who was at his door. Break-ins and thieves were just not common in the area, and if it was a bill collector, well, he'd just have to reason with him.

With all the possibilities that went through his mind, Will had to admit that not once had he considered that he'd find Cassidy on his doorstep when he threw open the front door.

"Something happen?" he asked, thinking only an emergency would bring her here.

Cassidy didn't bother answering his question. "Most

people around here still say 'hello' when they see some-one standing on their doorstep."

She waited for Will to step back and admit her. When he didn't, she ducked in around him.

"Maybe that's because most people don't see you on their doorstep," Will answered.

Since she'd walked in, he closed the door, resigned to her presence. Will braced himself, waiting for her to say something cryptic about his lack of housekeeping.

"How would you know?" Cassidy asked, looking around. She couldn't recall a single instance when she and her brothers had been inside Will's house. She could see why. The place looked positively depressing, she thought. "Have you asked around?"

What was she doing here? It wasn't as if she was in the habit of dropping by for a friendly visit. None of his friends ever did. His father's ranch had always been off-limits to them. His father always made a point of saying that.

"Is it Adam?" Will pressed. "Did something happen to Adam?" His mind raced through a list of possibilities. It had been almost three weeks since they'd rescued the boy, definitely time enough for word about him to get out. "Did his parents turn up?"

"No, nothing happened to Adam and no, his par-ents haven't turned up yet," she replied, answering Will's questions in order. She couldn't keep her reac-tion to herself any longer. "My Lord, it's gloomy in here. You might want to think about having a bigger window put in the front," she suggested, walking over to the rather small window that was there now, looking out on the front of the house. "Cole could help you with that. He's good with his hands." She glanced at Will over her shoulder. "A little more light coming in could only help."

She was making his head spin, not exactly an uncommon reaction whenever he was around Cassidy. He hadn't slept much last night after going over his finances and finding that the ranch his father had left to him was in even worse shape than he'd originally thought.

Cassidy was only adding to the headache he'd had ever since he'd gotten up.

Will caught hold of her shoulders, anchoring her in place so that he could get her to hopefully give him a straight answer.

"Cassidy, *why* are you here?" As he put the question to her, it occurred to him that she had asked him the same thing when he'd first gone over to her family ranch to pitch in with the baby.

But she had no such excuse. The baby wasn't here, only an ever-growing pile of bills and a mushrooming sense of impending failure.

"I guess you forgot. I figured you would," she told him.

He was having trouble hanging on to his temper right now. It felt as if the walls were closing in on him and his normal ability to take things in stride was seriously depleted. "Humor me. Tell me again."

Maybe it was the lack of light within the room, but he could have sworn there was a hint of amusement in those blue eyes of hers. Amusement and something else he couldn't quite read.

Just what was going on here?

"Okay," Cassidy said gamely, deciding to take him off the hook and answer his question. "I told you that I'd come over on the weekend to give you a hand on the ranch. I couldn't come last week or the week before that, but that doesn't mean I forgot about it. I live up to my promises—even if you don't think so," she told him pointedly.

He barely remembered the conversation. It felt almost like a lifetime ago, and while he'd enjoyed the handful of times he'd gone over to her ranch to help take care of Adam, it seemed like a pleasant interlude in an otherwise oppressive existence.

"That's okay. I absolve you of your hasty promise," Will told her, waving her words away. "Go home to the baby."

Cassidy dug in, her body language telling him that she wasn't going anywhere. "I said I'd give you a hand and I—"

"I don't need a hand," Will told her curtly, his patience snapping. "I need a miracle."

She was accustomed to bantering with him. At other times, biting words were exchanged between them as they bickered. But this was something different. His tone was different, almost hopeless, she realized. Cassidy couldn't recall ever seeing him like this. She wasn't about to walk away without some sort of an explanation from him.

"Define miracle," she told him. When he didn't answer her, Cassidy tried another approach. "Okay, what is it that you need done?"

"Go home, Cassidy," Will told her flatly. "There's nothing you can do."

She was used to him underestimating her. What she wasn't used to was not getting angry over it. Something about his manner kept her calm. What she felt was a genuine concern that he had a real problem.

"You'd be surprised at what I can do," she answered loftily. "Now I said I didn't intend to be in debt to you, and I'm not, so out with it," she instructed. "Just what kind of 'miracle' are you talking about?"

He looked at her as if she had lost her mind—or maybe he'd lost his and he was only imagining her here like this, trying to help him instead of trying to make his life miserable as was her usual custom.

Part of him thought that maybe this was some kind of an elaborate ruse on Cassidy's part to get him to believe that she actually wanted to help—just so she could laugh in his face when he told her what was wrong.

But then apathy came over him. What did it matter if she knew? Nothing was going to change. In the last couple of days, he'd woken up feeling numb, the way a man did when he knew he was going to go down for the third and last time because it was inevitable that he was going to drown.

Exasperated, Will blew out a breath and told her, "If I don't raise this month's mortgage payment, the bank is going to foreclose on the ranch."

Cassidy never took her eyes off his face as he talked. "And you don't want them to."

"Of course I don't want them to!" he shouted at her.

Why would he be this upset if losing the ranch didn't matter to him?

Someone else would have backed off, but Cassidy wasn't someone else.

"Why?" she questioned, trying to get him to talk to her, to tell her what he really felt. "Why not let the bank take it? This place only reminds you of your father," she pointed out.

"It also reminds me of other things," he told her. He didn't know why he was bothering to explain this to her. After all, she didn't care. But he still heard himself telling her, "Besides, if I let them foreclose, then he wins. The old man wins," he bit out. "He left this place to me only to yank it away after he died."

Cassidy could see that the bad blood between Will and his father ran deep. "That's giving him a lot of credit for thinking clearly," she said, and then she shook her head because he probably wasn't aware of this. "Your father wasn't thinking clearly toward the end."

Will didn't ask her for details. He didn't want to know. Knowing would only compound the feeling of depression and hopelessness he was trying hard to battle and keep at bay.

He had to find a way to rally, to come up with a way to make the mortgage payment so he could buy himself some time until he could turn the ranch into a paying enterprise again.

Will had fallen silent. Cassidy tried prodding him again. "How much do you need?"

His eyes met hers. "Why?" he challenged.

Since he didn't seem to believe that she wanted to

help him—he was, after all, her brothers' friend—she went back to the persona he felt he did know. "Because I want to know what it takes to make you go under."

Will squared his shoulders. It gave her hope. "I'm not going under."

"So back to my question. How much do you need?" she asked again.

He knew that she wasn't going to let up until he finally told her what she wanted to know.

So, grudgingly, he did.

Cassidy nodded. "Okay," was all she said in response as she turned on her heel and headed for the front door.

"I thought you said you came to help," he called after her. It was meant to mock her because he'd never expected her to stay and work on the ranch no matter what she'd initially said to the contrary.

"I did," she told him. And then, just as she opened the door to go out, Cassidy surprised him by adding, "I am."

And with that, she left.

"Right."

Will shook his head. That seemed par for the course, he thought, staring at the closed door.

He didn't have time to think about Cassidy and why she was behaving even stranger than usual. He had horses to feed. At least that much he could do. Coming up with that miracle he needed, however, was another story entirely.

INSTEAD OF GOING back home to share what she'd managed to get out of Will with her brothers, Cassidy went straight to town. Specifically, she went straight to Miss Joan's diner.

The diner was full when she walked in. On weekends, people had a few more minutes to spare on breakfast, or at least their morning coffee, than they did on weekday mornings.

Despite the crowd, Miss Joan spotted her before she had walked more than two feet into the diner.

Their eyes meeting, Miss Joan beckoned her over to the counter. The older woman had a cup of coffee waiting for her by the time she reached it.

"Light," Miss Joan said, pushing the cup toward her. "Just like you like it. Now take a load off and tell me what's bothering you."

While Miss Joan's voice couldn't exactly be described as inviting, it had been known to coax many a story from a troubled soul.

Cassidy sat down at the counter. She knew better than to hesitate. Miss Joan wasn't a person someone played games with.

She told Miss Joan everything, that she'd come straight from Will's ranch, adding that she'd never seen him like that before. "He was so incredibly disheartened, he was almost like another person."

"Go on," Miss Joan urged quietly.

Cassidy went on to say she thought that Will was almost on the brink of defeat. She'd also told her why. Miss Joan listened and nodded. She waved off another customer when that man called out to her to get her attention.

Her eyes were fixed on Cassidy. "How much did you say he needed?"

Cassidy repeated the sum, remembering when an extra dollar could make all the difference in the world. "I know that in the scheme of things, it might not sound like all that much," she told Miss Joan, "but—"

"But when you don't have it, it's a king's ransom," Miss Joan concluded knowingly. She leaned closer to Cassidy, her words intended for the young woman's ears only. "I've been running this diner a lot of years now, and I've always been a woman with simple needs. I've got more money than I could even spend. If I lent Will the money for his ranch—"

Cassidy shook her head. She knew Will, knew how he thought. "He wouldn't accept it," she told her.

The hint of a smile on the woman's thin lips told Cassidy that she already knew that.

"What would you suggest?" Miss Joan asked, wanting to see if they were of a like mind.

She'd been mulling over possible solutions ever since she'd left Will's ranch. "We could start a fundraiser," Cassidy proposed. "Get everyone to put in a little. That way it's from everybody, not just one person. He couldn't turn that down."

Miss Joan laughed at the certainty she heard in Cassidy's voice. "Do you *know* Will Laredo?" she asked.

"Okay, he could turn it down," Cassidy allowed, then added fiercely, "But I won't let him. If he lets that ranch go, it'll eat at him for the rest of his life—and that's just not going to happen."

Miss Joan nodded, pleased to hear Cassidy take this stand. She was pleased for a number of reasons, not the least of which was that she had a feeling in her bones that all those years that Cassidy and Will had spent feuding and sniping at each other were about to come to a long anticipated end.

About time, Miss Joan thought.

Picking up a thick water glass, Miss Joan began to hit its side with a knife. She kept on hitting it until the noise level within the diner died down and then completely faded away.

"I'd like everyone's attention," she declared in her honey-dipped whiskey voice.

And once she was satisfied that she had it, Miss Joan launched into the details of why she was holding an impromptu fund-raiser at the diner, explaining that no one was going to be allowed to leave without contributing *something*.

It didn't matter how little, but it had to be something.

She went on to add—without mentioning a name— that this was for one of their own, and that each and every one of them—herself included—knew what it was like to be faced with bills that couldn't be paid on time for one reason or another.

To seal the deal, Miss Joan told the diner patrons that if they could afford it and their contribution was for a decent amount, they would receive a voucher for a free breakfast on the date of their choice.

And then Miss Joan sat back and waited.

She didn't have long to wait.

"You're back," Will said in surprise late that same afternoon.

Cassidy had spotted him in the corral. After parking her truck near the ranch house, she'd walked back to where he was working with the horses that Connor had told her Will had bought earlier in the month. Ironically, it was with the last of his money.

She wasted no time with small talk. Instead, she crossed over to Will and ordered, "Put out your hands."

"Why?" he asked warily, eyeing the sack she was carrying.

Cassidy huffed. "Will you stop questioning everything I say, and for once in your life just do as I ask?"

After a moment, Will put out one hand. The wary look in his eyes, however, remained.

Cassidy frowned. Even when it was a good deed, it was like pulling teeth with this man. "Both of them," she prompted.

He regarded Cassidy suspiciously, then did as she asked, never taking his eyes off her.

She opened the sack and took out a manila envelope, holding it out to him. The envelope looked as if it was about to burst.

Will made no move to undo the clasp. Instead, he asked, "What is this?"

"The miracle you asked for," she answered very simply.

When he said nothing, only continued looking at it, she scowled at him. "You do have a way of sucking the joy out of things, you know that? Take it. It's the money you said you needed to keep the bank from foreclosing on the ranch."

Instead of accepting it, Will pushed the envelope back toward her. "I can't take your money."

Cassidy pushed it right back at him. "It's not my money."

"Well, then I can't take Connor's money," he said, impatience mounting in his voice.

"It's not his, either." She saw him open his mouth. "And before you go down the list, it's not Cody's or Cole's, either."

She was playing games again. No one he knew had that kind of money to lend him just like that. "Then whose is it?"

"Yours," she answered innocently.

"Cassidy," he warned, "don't play games with me."

"Trust me, the last thing on my mind is playing with you, Laredo," she told him. It was clear that she was not about to tell him the origin of the money. She didn't want anything getting in the way of his accepting the money and saving his ranch. "Consider this an early Christmas present. Now stop being a jackass and take this to the bank. You've got just enough time before it closes to make that payment. Unless, of course, you want your father to be right—posthumously."

Cassidy had always known just what to say in order to goad him.

"This isn't over," Will promised her, taking the money.

"I didn't think it was," she told him, adding with a smile, "I look forward to round two."

Chapter Thirteen

"I don't get it," Will said to Connor.

Several days had passed since Cassidy had brought him the mysterious envelope filled with money, and this was the first opportunity that the two of them had to get together. Connor had come by Will's ranch to volunteer his help, taking his turn the same way that his siblings were doing.

The first thing Will did was tell him about the envelope full of cash that Cassidy had given him.

"I've asked around, but nobody'll tell me where that money came from," Will said, clearly confounded as to the money's origin.

Because Cassidy knew she could trust him—and because she hadn't wanted him thinking that she had bent some laws to secure the funds—his sister had confided in him about Miss Joan's impromptu fund-raiser for Will's mortgage payment.

He and Will were working on replacing several lengths of fencing that composed the corral. It was almost restored.

"You don't have a need to know," Connor told him.

"All that matters is that you bought yourself some time with the money."

"I know that," Will answered impatiently, holding the rail steady as Connor nailed the new length to the end that remained on that side. "But, Connor, in all good conscience—"

Finished hammering that end, Connor let the hammer drop before he tested the strength of the replaced rail. "Will, conscience has a place in our lives, a very big place. But sometimes, you just have to close your eyes and go on faith," he told his friend.

Will wasn't sure if he could accept that. Most of all, he wasn't sure just how to interpret Cassidy's actions. "Just what the hell is your sister up to?" he asked.

"Who knows? This is Cassidy we're talking about," he reminded Will. "She's always been rather unpredictable. Maybe *she's* following her conscience." Connor stopped working and faced the other man. "Look, she did a good deed. Let it go at that. You two have spent so much time bickering, you completely lost sight of the two human beings living behind all that rhetoric."

Pausing, Connor stooped to pick up his hammer again. "Now, are we going to spend the rest of the day flapping our gums, getting nowhere, or are we going to get some work done?" he asked. "'Cause I am *not* a man of leisure and this is all the time I can spare for a while."

Will nodded. Connor was right. His father had left the family ranch not just in debt but in complete disrepair, and he was grateful for any help he could get. "Work," he answered.

Connor smiled, patting his friend's back. "Good choice."

"Still want to know where she got that money," Will murmured as he picked up another length of railing.

"I'm sure you do," Connor replied mildly as he began hammering again.

The inference was clear. There were more important things that needed his friend's attention than discovering where the money had come from.

Cassidy was running behind.

Actually, these last few weeks, she felt as if she was always running and always behind, she thought as she hastily buttoned her blouse. She couldn't remember ever feeling this tired.

She supposed that this was what it felt like to be a single mother, always trying to balance taking care of a baby with the demands of a job—except that she wasn't a single mother. She wasn't a mother at all. Any day now, all that would change, and her life would slow down and get back to normal, whatever that was.

What really surprised her was that the thought wasn't nearly as comforting as she'd expected it to be.

Hurrying into the rest of her clothes, Cassidy winced when she heard Adam beginning to cry.

Again.

She stopped by his crib, which was a few feet away from her bed and the chief reason why she wasn't getting anything close to a full night's sleep since he'd taken up temporary residency in her house.

Though she tried not to be, Cassidy was tuned in to

Adam's every movement and was aware of each time he so much as shifted in his crib whether he was asleep or not.

"I've already fed you and changed you. *Why* are you crying?" she asked the baby helplessly.

Cody's wife had volunteered to watch the baby today, but she couldn't very well leave Devon with a crying baby, especially when her own baby had turned into a dynamo who was just beginning to crawl and get into everything.

"Okay, tell me what's wrong?" Cassidy asked wearily, picking Adam up. She had her answer immediately. The baby felt as if he was on fire. "Oh, my God, you're hot. Really hot. You weren't this hot half an hour ago." She could feel herself beginning to panic. "I didn't know anyone could get this hot so fast."

As fear enveloped her, Cassidy felt as if she wanted to run in half a dozen directions all at the same time. She tried to focus and found that she really couldn't.

Grabbing her shoes, Cassidy all but flew down the stairs, holding the wailing baby against her. "Connor," she cried, raising her voice so she could be heard above the baby's wails.

Reaching the bottom of the stairs, she looked around desperately, trying to locate her oldest brother. When she didn't see or hear him, she dashed into the kitchen and all but crashed into him there.

Connor was just putting dishes into the dishwasher.

"What's wrong?" The trivial guess he was about to make to answer his own question faded the second he saw the look on his sister's face. He'd never seen her like that before. "Cassidy?" he asked uncertainly.

"It's the baby," she cried, her voice almost breaking. "Connor, he's burning up."

He was accustomed to hearing his sister exaggerating things, but when he took the baby from her—wanting to comfort both of them—he could feel the heat radiating from Adam.

For once, Cassidy *wasn't* exaggerating. "You're right," he told her, cradling the unhappy baby against him. "He is hot."

"I know I'm right," she answered impatiently. "What do I do?" Connor was the one they all turned to for advice, the one they depended on. "Is it even possible to be this hot without— What do I do?" she repeated, not wanting to complete the thought that had just flashed through her head.

"We need to get him to the clinic," Connor told her.

He was doing his best to keep the urgency out of his voice because he didn't want to make Cassidy any more panicked than she already was, but one look into her eyes and he knew that she saw through his act.

"It's bad, isn't it?" she asked him, trying hard not to allow her fear to get the better of her.

"You ran high fevers all the time when you were around his size. You nearly drove Dad crazy. Turns out you're still here," he pointed out comfortingly. "But it never hurts to have a doctor check him out. At least we won't have to drive fifty miles to Mission Ridge the way we did when you were running high fevers. There was no clinic in town when you were Adam's age.

"C'mon, let's go," he said, walking ahead of her with the baby.

It was all Cassidy could do to remember to grab her purse before she hurried after him. Her brain felt like the contents of a scattered can of green peas.

"So HE'LL BE all right?" Cassidy asked Dr. Alisha Murphy anxiously, wanting to hear the pediatrician reassure her again.

Alisha smiled. "He'll be fine. Babies run high fevers all the time," she said. There was nothing but sympathy in her voice as she looked down at her little patient. "But just to be sure, why don't I keep this little trouper here today for observation? This way I can check in on him every half hour or so to make sure everything's under control. I'll have Debi give you a call if there's any significant change."

Cassidy was torn.

She thought of all the files she'd allowed to pile up on her desk in the office these last few weeks. She didn't want Olivia or Cash to feel that she was letting them down. She was trying to forge a career, which meant she needed to act accordingly, not appear as if she was just going through the motions when it suited her. But at the same time, she wanted to be here, with Adam. He needed her, and she needed to be reassured that he wasn't going to take a turn for the worse. She was well aware that things had a way of changing suddenly, especially at that age.

Finally, she relented. "All right," Cassidy agreed,

then added, "As long as you're sure someone will call me if Adam suddenly starts getting worse."

"He won't, but one of us will definitely call you if anything changes," Alisha promised, then added comfortingly, "Kids are a lot more resilient than we think they are, and this little guy seemed like he was a healthy baby the last time I examined him."

Taking the words to heart, Cassidy finally left the clinic.

She wondered how mothers did it, how they made it intact through their baby's first year. It had to be extremely taxing, not to mention exhausting. How did they do it? And how did they, knowing all this, go on to have more children? It seemed like a mystery to her, she thought, leaving the clinic.

CASSIDY COULDN'T REMEMBER the last time a day had gone by so slowly. She checked her watch as well as her phone periodically, afraid she'd somehow missed a call. But other than a call from each of her brothers and her sister-in-law, checking on how the baby was doing as well as how *she* was doing, there were no other calls.

Specifically, there were no calls from the clinic requesting her immediate presence.

Eventually Cassidy calmed down enough to concentrate on her work—at least to a degree.

And the minute that her workday was officially over, Cassidy was out of the office and the one-story building like a shot. Since Connor had driven her to the clinic, she had no means of transportation available. He had gone back to the ranch, leaving specific instructions that she call him the minute she was ready to pick up the baby and come home.

She wasn't about to bother him until she knew what was going on, so she walked to the clinic now, after turning down both Cash's and Olivia's offer to drive her there. She insisted she was quite capable of getting there on her own.

Because the town was small, everything was within walking distance, although she had to concede that some of those distances were farther than others.

Besides, she'd told Olivia, she could use the exercise to walk off her tension. Her boss had decided not to argue the point.

When she walked into the clinic, Cassidy saw that Debi was behind the reception desk. The woman looked up as she entered and waved her into the back.

"Dr. Alisha's just checking on Adam," the nurse told her. "You can go right in."

Wanting to race to the last exam room—which had been converted to an interim hospital room where patients could recover from minor outpatient surgery—Cassidy still hesitated at the closed door. She needed a second to brace herself before entering.

Once she walked in, she asked Alisha, "How's he doing?"

The pediatrician smiled at her patient's "mother," obviously happy about being able to deliver a positive prognosis.

"He's doing better. His fever's almost gone, but it's still hanging in there to some degree."

Was the doctor deliberately keeping something from

her? Cassidy wondered. Her stomach had been queasy all day, ever since she'd realized that Adam's fever had spiked.

"Give it to me straight, Doc. Should I be worried?" Cassidy asked.

Alisha met the question with a self-depreciating laugh. "Mothers go on worrying until after their kids turn fifty. After that, they still worry, but I hear not as much," she confided, then went on to say, "Because this is his first go-round with a high fever, I'm going to suggest keeping him here overnight."

Cassidy felt a rush of disappointment. "Then I can't take him home?"

"You could," Alisha conjectured, "but if the fever suddenly goes up again for some reason, you're going to have to drive back here, and I promise you that you'll agonize all the way. This way, he'll be right here, and if his fever does spike for some reason, which is only a possibility, not a sure thing, I can give him a shot to bring it down again."

Cassidy felt as if she needed everything spelled out for her. "But the fever's down now, right?"

"It's down," Alisha assured her.

Cassidy chewed on her bottom lip, undecided as to what to do for a moment. And then she looked up. "How about a compromise?" she proposed. "Adam will stay here overnight, but I'll stay with him, not you. If anything goes wrong, I'll call you or Dr. Dan right away." She could see that the doctor was about to protest the decision. "You need to go home to your own kids, Doc. They probably don't see you nearly enough."

"All right. Either one of us can be here within minutes," she stated.

Cassidy nodded. She really hadn't wanted to leave Adam's side, anyway. She'd spent every night for the last month near him, and she wouldn't be able to sleep at all knowing he was sick somewhere away from her. "Good enough for me, Doc."

Alisha eyed her rather warily. "Are you sure about this?"

Cassidy never hesitated. "I'm very sure," she said firmly.

ALISHA ASKED HER the same question a few hours later as she was about to close the clinic for the night. Cassidy gave her the same answer.

"Okay, then I'll see you in the morning," Alisha told her, softly closing the door behind her.

After checking on Adam, who was mercifully asleep and breathing a lot better, at least for the time being, Cassidy noted, she sat back down in the chair.

She wasn't aware of sighing as she tried to find a comfortable position for herself in order to settle in for the night.

Just as she was about to close her eyes, Cassidy heard the door behind her opening again. It had only been a few minutes since the doctor had left her.

"I said I'm sure," Cassidy repeated, hoping that would finally send the doctor on her way to her own family for the night.

"What are you sure about?"

Only extreme restraint kept her for crying out in surprise.

As it was, Cassidy jumped to her feet, almost sending the chair crashing to the floor. Will darted in and caught it just in time.

"What are you doing here, Laredo?" she asked. "It's after hours, and everyone at the clinic's gone home for the night."

"Yes, I know," Will told her. "I passed Dr. Alisha just as she was locking up. She was the one who let me in."

Cassidy pulled him over, away from the sleeping baby before his voice could wake Adam up.

"I repeat," she said to him in an annoyed whisper, "what are you doing here?"

"I'm here so you can get some rest. We can take turns watching the baby while the other one sleeps."

As far as she knew, none of her brothers had called him about Adam's fever. At least, none of them had mentioned it to her. But that didn't mean that they hadn't. She frowned.

"How did you find out he was sick?" she asked. If she had to make a guess, she supposed that Connor had to have told him, but she guessed wrong.

The answer was quite simple. "Miss Joan told me when I stopped by the diner on my way back from the general store."

Cassidy sighed. She didn't bother asking how Miss Joan had found out. Miss Joan *always* found out.

"So how is he?" Will asked, nodding toward the baby.

"Better," Cassidy answered. "His fever's almost gone

Look, you don't have to stay here with me, taking turns watching him. I can—"

"I wasn't asking for permission," Will pointed out quietly. "We both rescued him. That means, like it or not, Cassidy, we're both in this together."

Cassidy sighed again. "You're determined to ignore me, aren't you?"

Will watched her for a long moment, so long that she could almost feel her body heating beneath his gaze. Cassidy upbraided herself for her reaction. She did her best not to look at the smile that was slowly slipping over his lips.

"Oh, I wouldn't say that," he said, more to himself than to her. He had finally come to terms with the fact that ignoring Cassidy was just not in the cards for him. "You look like you've been through the wringer. I'll spell you for an hour." He dragged over another chair and positioning it on the other side of the crib that had been brought in for the baby.

He was about to tell her that she could close her eyes now and discovered that he didn't have to. She already had.

Chapter Fourteen

Cassidy's eyes flew open as if someone had shaken her shoulder to rouse her. As far as she could tell, only a few minutes had passed since she'd closed her eyes.

Taking a deep breath, she tried to orient herself a little more. She focused in on her watch to make sure that she *hadn't* been asleep for long.

A moment later, she remembered why she was here—and with whom.

"Sorry," she murmured, certain that he'd noticed that her eyes had closed. "I was just resting my eyes for a minute."

"You were asleep," Will corrected her with a grin. "But let's not quibble over terms."

"I wasn't quibbling, I was 'stating,'" she told him emphatically. "In this case, stating the fact that I wasn't asleep." Knowing Will, he'd take her momentary catnap as an opportunity to ridicule her about it, or something along those lines.

He hadn't come here to argue, Will thought. He'd come here to help—no matter how much she fought him about it.

"Fine, have it your way," he allowed. "I'm really not in the mood for another battle of 'who gets the last word' with you. I'm just here to help."

She couldn't help it. She was very suspicious of this so-called act of kindness on Will's part. She recalled the state of his range.

"Don't you have enough to do?" she asked.

His eyes met hers, and she had that same feeling that he was looking deep into her thoughts, her soul, that she'd had before.

"Well, thanks to the last person in the world I ever thought would volunteer to help me, I seem to have gotten a stay of execution, so right now I have a little extra time to spare, and this is where I want to be, watching over Adam."

She wasn't just going to allow him to take over like that. Cassidy knew him. She'd be pushed over to the sidelines in no time flat.

"I'm watching over Adam," she told him.

He could work with that. "And I'm watching you watching over Adam," he amended.

Cassidy had a feeling that this could go on forever, and she knew it wasn't really getting either one of them anywhere. Besides, she had to admit—if only to herself and certainly not out loud—that she was rather touched that Laredo was so concerned about the boy's condition. Adam had gotten to both of them.

It started her thinking about the whole situation again. And that aroused a fresh set of fears.

"You know, I've kind of gotten used to having him

around." She sighed, pressing her lips together. "It's probably a bad thing."

Will's forehead furrowed as he looked at her. "Why would you say that?"

"Because I'm really going to miss him when his parents show up to take him." She felt a pang even as she said the words.

"I'm not so sure they're ever going to." When she looked at him quizzically, he said, "Think about it. It's been a month since that flood hit, and so far, nobody has come forward looking for him. Not even after we took him with us to the reservation."

"Maybe they can't come forward," she suggested. "Maybe Adam's parents are in the hospital, in a coma, recovering from a car accident or some other kind of unforeseen mishap."

There was one problem with her theory. "Are you forgetting the closest hospital is fifty miles away?" he reminded her.

She was still casting about, trying to find a viable excuse. What she couldn't bring herself to believe was that Adam had been abandoned.

"Maybe whoever they were with, or his mother was with, realized how badly they were—or she was—hurt and took them straight to Mission Ridge and the hospital."

"And the baby? How do you explain the baby being out there in the flash flood?" he asked.

She was working hard to try to pull all the ends together. Although she'd always maintained that she didn't have any maternal feelings, she'd been trying to see what happened from her own point of view.

"The flash flood hit suddenly, she wanted to save the baby so she put him into that plastic thing we found him in. Meanwhile, she got swept away and lost consciousness. Then someone found her. When she remained unresponsive, they took her to the hospital."

Listening to her, Will could only shake his head. "Incredible."

"You like that, huh?" Cassidy asked proudly, happy that she was able to come up with a scenario that seemed to account for all the pieces.

He hadn't meant that her explanation was incredible. The word was meant to describe her and the contortions her mind had gone to in order to come up with this convoluted explanation.

"I'll say this for you," he said, laughing shortly, "you've got one hell of an imagination."

It wasn't hard to read between the lines. "So you don't think that's possible?" she asked him, taking offense.

"If you've taught me nothing else, Cassidy, you've taught me that just about anything *could be* possible," he told her.

Cassidy frowned at him. "You're being sarcastic again," she accused.

"No, actually," he stated, "I'm being in awe. I've honestly never seen anyone bob and weave the way you do. Who knows? The sheriff still hasn't found either a body or an abandoned car, so until one or the other—

or both—turn up, then I guess that anything *could* be possible in these circumstances."

In light of what she'd just suggested, Cassidy thought that perhaps another course of action was necessary. "Maybe the sheriff should place a call to the Mission Ridge Hospital."

"Actually, I think he is, first thing in the morning," Will said.

This was news to her. "You talked with him," she assumed.

Will had stopped by the sheriff's office just before coming to the clinic. "Just to find out if he was making any progress locating Adam's parents," Will told her. "He hasn't, so after we talked, contacting the hospital is what he's going to try next."

She nodded, thinking about the possible end result of the sheriff's investigation—either end. "What if he doesn't find anyone?" she asked.

"You're talking about Adam's parents?"

"Right. What if Sheriff Santiago calls all the local hospitals in a hundred-mile radius and doesn't find anyone who could possibly be Adam's parents, then what? What happens to Adam?"

"Exactly what would have happened to him if you hadn't stepped up and volunteered to take him until his parents—or mother—could be located. He'll be sent to social services in Mission Ridge—or maybe even one of the larger cities—and then they'll place him in someone's home."

The very suggestion of Adam being taken away to live with someone else made her blood run cold. "And you'd be okay with that?" she challenged, horrified at the thought of Adam being passed from hand to hand, without anyone actually caring for the boy.

"I didn't say that," Will corrected her tersely. "But there's not exactly a lot that I can do in this situation. I can't claim I have some kind of blood relationship with him, and I'm sure that nobody would let *me* adopt him."

She listened to Will, surprised that he had actually thought it out that far. Maybe she'd misjudged him after all.

"Social services wants a stable home environment for any child they place. Considering that I was on the brink of foreclosure, and if I don't wind up selling a few of the horses and start making some kind of profit, no matter how minor, I'll wind up losing the ranch, I'm not exactly a star candidate. Social services doesn't smile upon a prospective adoptive parent living out of his truck."

She pushed aside all that, wanting to be perfectly clear about what he was saying. "But otherwise, you would?"

He'd lost the thread of what she was saying to him. Cassidy had a way of jumping around. "What?"

She tried to be clearer. "Otherwise, if the ranch didn't go into foreclosure and you were making a go of it, you would adopt Adam?"

Will didn't even pause to think about it. He knew what he would do. "Sure, why not?"

Cassidy had to admit that she was having trouble wrapping her mind around this new, improved Will Laredo. "I've got a better question for you—why? Why would you adopt Adam?"

"Maybe so I could give him a home, give him someone who cared about him. And maybe, while we're at it, so I could finally have a family myself." Maybe it was the late hour, or the situation, or just a combination of both. Whatever it was, he found himself admitting things to Cassidy that he had never said out loud before. "I never felt I had one before. The closest I ever came to feeling like I had a family was when I hung around your brothers and you."

That really took her aback. "I understand you feeling that way about my brothers, but about me, too?" she questioned.

Will shrugged. "Sure, a lot of brothers have pesky little sisters. Your brothers certainly did," he pointed out with a grin.

Cassidy drew herself up. "I was never a pesky little sister to them," she protested.

Will laughed. He could think of so many different instances to cite. "Right. You keep telling yourself that."

"I wasn't," she insisted. "We were a team, my brothers and I. We had to be once Dad was gone, we had to work together to make a go of the ranch. Otherwise, the county was going to come in and take us away. At least take three of us away," she amended.

Will nodded, vividly remembering how concerned Connor had been that he might not get custody of his siblings. Never once had he lamented about what he was giving up for them.

"Yes, I remember. I guess, in a way, that gives the three of us something in common," Will said, nodding at the baby and then her.

Ordinarily Cassidy would have protested the comparison, saying that while she and the baby had something in common, when it came to running the very real danger of having the county step in and absorb them, she and Will had *nothing* in common. But it wasn't true. She and Will were both orphans, she because her parents had both died and he because, while his father had remained alive for a lot of years after hers had passed away, Will had been just as alone as they were. His father had died on the inside long before the man was officially pronounced dead on the outside.

Though she would have hated to admit it, she could feel herself empathizing with Will. All she was willing to do was vaguely say, "I guess it does."

Will did his best to suppress a grin. "I guess I must be the one who's asleep."

Cassidy stared at him, trying to fathom his meaning. "What are you talking about?"

He tried again. "Well, I must be asleep because I'm definitely dreaming."

Still nothing. "Again, *what*?" Cassidy said impatiently.

"I'm dreaming," Will repeated. "You're being much too agreeable for this to actually be taking place. The Cassidy McCullough I know enjoys vivisecting me with her tongue. The one I think I'm talking to is being sweet, kind and understanding."

Was that a backhanded compliment—or a backhanded insult? She wasn't sure. "I can start vivisecting again if you'd prefer."

"No, that's okay," he quickly assured her with a laugh. "Let me go on dreaming a little longer."

Cassidy could only sigh. "You're crazy, you know that, don't you?"

"For what I'm thinking?" His eyes slid along the length of her, saying things to her that were better left unsaid—for both their sakes. "Yeah, probably," Will agreed.

Cassidy couldn't explain why, but she felt this warm shiver undulating up and down her spine like a garden snake uncoiling and staking out its territory while it was familiarizing itself with its new surroundings.

She did what she could to block the sensation, but for some reason, that only seemed to reinforce it.

"I'm not interested in what you're thinking," she finally said in a last-ditch effort to make Will think that his words—and the intent behind them—left her completely cold instead of the exact opposite.

"That's good," he replied, his voice mild. "Because I'm not about to tell you."

And that simple declaration aroused her curiosity. "Why not?"

"Because it wouldn't be safe."

"For me?" she challenged. Only she was the best judge of what was—or wasn't—safe for her to hear. He had no right to make that judgment call, and she was about to make him know it—never mind that something was warning her that she was heading into dangerous territory.

The smile that was teasing the corners of his mouth—

and consequently her—made her stomach feel as if it was filling up with wall-to-wall butterflies.

Cassidy reminded herself that she'd been so worried about Adam and his fever that she hadn't eaten all day. *That* was to blame for the tight, twisted feeling in the pit of her stomach, nothing else.

Certainly not Will Laredo.

"No," Will contradicted her, "it wouldn't be safe for me."

She scowled at him. "Even when you're being supposedly 'nice,' you manage to make me want to strangle you," she told him.

The smile on Will's face only widened. "Good to know."

Her eyes darkened. "That wasn't meant to be a compliment."

"My mistake," he said. His tone told her that he felt the exact opposite.

Damn it, he wasn't getting to her. He *wasn't*, Cassidy silently insisted. It was just a matter of too little sleep and nothing to eat. And no coffee. Agitated about Adam, she hadn't had her morning coffee. She *always* had her morning coffee, or nothing was in sync for her all day long.

Tomorrow would be better, Cassidy promised herself. Tomorrow she would see this evening for what it was: a fluke, an aberration. A product of a number of minuses, nothing more.

"Well, if you're not going to go to sleep, then I am," she announced.

His smile was nothing if not encouraging. She just *had* to stop letting it get to her.

"That's what I've been telling you to do all along," Will said.

"I'm not doing it because you're telling me to," she informed him. "I'm doing it because it's just a huge waste for both of us to be staying awake like this."

Will spread his hands wide, amused. "My thoughts exactly."

"Stop being so agreeable, Laredo," she snapped. He was putting her on edge, behaving like this. "That's not like you."

That damn sexy smile was back, undulating under her skin, causing more havoc.

"Maybe it is."

She would have let out a scream if it wouldn't have woken up the baby. As it was, it was difficult to conduct an argument in whispers, especially when one of the two people in the argument refused to argue.

She didn't like these new rules. "You're just messing with my mind," Cassidy accused.

Will inclined his head. "If you say so."

She clenched her hands in her lap, curling her fingernails into her palms. She was doing what she could in order to ground herself.

This wasn't getting her anywhere.

Maybe a little reverse psychology might help her out. "Anyway, thanks for trying to spell me."

"Operative word here being *trying*. Thank me once I succeed," he told her, sounding almost annoyingly cheerful.

It told her that he was enjoying this, enjoying getting under her skin, getting in the last word, because that was the way Laredo was built. You couldn't change the spots on a leopard, she insisted. Even a leopard with a very sexy smile.

Especially a leopard with a very sexy smile.

Chapter Fifteen

Will was gone.

When Cassidy opened her eyes again, she looked directly across from where she was sitting to the chair on the other side of the crib and saw that it was empty.

Her eyes swept over the small room with the same results. Will was nowhere to be found.

Adam, mercifully, appeared to be sleeping comfortably. Had he slept quietly through the night? Or had she, for the first time in four weeks, just slept right through his cries?

She noticed the empty formula bottle on the counter and saw that the seal on the pack of disposable diapers the doctor had left had been broken. Sometime during the night, Adam had been changed and fed—and she had slept right through it.

"After all this time, Will Laredo, you've actually managed to surprise me," she murmured, shaking her head. Who knew?

A noise coming from the front of the clinic caught Cassidy's attention. Thinking that Will was out there, trying to scrounge up some coffee in the minuscule break room, she went out, intending to ask him why he hadn't woken her up to take care of the baby.

But again, she didn't find Will.

Instead, she found Holly, the clinic's other nurse, making coffee in the alcove that was right off the reception area.

Holly swung around the second that she walked into the alcove.

"Oh, Cassidy, you startled me," Holly cried. "I forgot that you were staying here overnight with the baby. How's he doing?" she asked. Putting down the coffee decanter, Holly suddenly appeared concerned. "His fever hasn't gone up again, has it?"

Not waiting for an answer, Holly went quickly to see for herself.

"No, it hasn't gone up," Cassidy called after her. "Adam's sleeping and his head feels cool, thank goodness."

Since she was already there, Holly tiptoed into the room and checked for herself, lightly brushing her fingertips across the baby's forehead.

Adam stirred a little but continued sleeping.

"You're right," Holly whispered as she slipped out of the room. "Cool as a cucumber." She smiled at Cassidy. "I think you've survived your first baby crisis."

Holly led the way back to the break room. "One of the doctors should be here soon. They all usually get in early," she told Cassidy. A smile played on her lips. "You'd think we liked it here, or something."

Cassidy watched as the nurse went back to making coffee. "When you first came in," she began, trying to sound as if she didn't care what the answer was one way or another, "you didn't happen to see anyone else here, did you?"

"Like who?" Holly asked. "Like I said, I'd forgotten about you and Adam staying overnight. Was there supposed to be someone else here, too? Because I didn't see anyone."

That was all she wanted to know. Cassidy shook her head. She definitely didn't want to get into an explanation. "Never mind."

If she said anything about Will being here through the night, Holly might get the wrong idea. That was how rumors started in a town the size of a postage stamp, a town where almost nothing ever happened. The least deviation from the norm and everyone jumped on it, hoping to sink their teeth into something of substance, or at the very least, something diverting.

She could see for herself that Will wasn't here, and if Holly wasn't saying anything, that meant that he had left before the nurse opened the clinic.

Cassidy glanced at her watch. It was barely 7:00 a.m.

How had she not heard Laredo leaving? she asked herself. Or, for that matter, how had she not heard Adam fussing? For the last month, she'd been tuned in to every sound that the baby made, so why was last night any different?

"When did you say that one of the doctors was coming in?" Cassidy asked, then added, "I'm assuming that one of them has to sign Adam out so it'll be okay for me to take him home."

Holly waved away Cassidy's concern. "I'm sure it's

okay to take him home since his fever's gone, but if you want to make it official, Dr. Dan or Dr. Alisha should be here anytime now."

The words were no sooner out of Holly's mouth than they heard the front door being opened.

"There's one of them now," Holly said. "Unless it's Debi," she amended.

But it wasn't Debi. It was Dan, in before eight as had become his habit ever since he'd reopened the clinic several years ago.

"So how's our patient doing?" he asked brightly the moment he saw Cassidy.

"Much better," she answered, relieved. "His fever's gone."

"Told you it would be," he reminded her. He and Alisha had taken turns checking on their littlest patient throughout the day. "Scary stuff the first time it happens, though. And the second, and the third. Gets a little better as time goes on, but never really easier. Worrying is just something you have to come to terms with and get used to."

Cassidy felt that the doctor was talking as if Adam was her baby instead of just a child she found temporarily in her care. She wanted to correct him and remind him that she wasn't really connected to Adam, but decided to let it go.

She played down the "worry" aspect by saying, "I just wanted you to look him over to make sure that I could take him home."

Except that it isn't his home, it's just his temporary

shelter, Cassidy reminded herself. She was guilty of making the same mistake that the doctor had just made.

But she had to admit that over the last month, she had come to regard Adam as her own. She knew she shouldn't, but that didn't change anything.

Dan delivered the same verdict that Holly had a few minutes earlier. The baby's fever was gone. Adam was as healthy as if yesterday had never happened.

"Take the boy home," Dan told her happily.

Although she already knew that the baby was all right, Cassidy still breathed a sigh of relief.

"Thank you!"

And then she put a call in to Connor.

"You're sure you don't mind?" she questioned her brother a little more than an hour later.

Connor had dropped everything and come for them the moment she'd called. They were home now, and her question referred to her leaving Adam in his care while she returned to town to run an errand.

"There're some papers I need to pick up from the office so I can work on them here, but maybe I can do that later—"

Connor nodded. Cassidy might very well be picking up files at the office, the way she said she needed to, but he had a hunch that those files weren't her main focus. He had known Cassidy her entire life—long enough and well enough to see through excuses when she came up with them—like now.

Something else was on her mind. He wasn't about

to ask her what, confident that when she wanted him to know, Cassidy would tell him.

"I'm sure. I was planning on working on the books today, anyway, so I'll only be a cry away if Adam wants something. Go, do whatever you have to do," he told her, waving his sister out the front door and on her way.

HER BROTHER HAD worded his sentence just vaguely enough—"Go do whatever you have to do"—for her to be able to hide a multitude of deeds within it.

Cassidy made sure she stopped at the law firm first. Something told her that if she left that errand for last, she might never make it to the office. Not that she was a slacker, or flighty, but she'd learned that things had a way of happening when she was around Laredo. Cassidy didn't want to chance not picking up what she wanted her brother to believe was essentially her "main reason" for leaving Adam and the ranch.

Laredo, or rather his ranch, was her next—and last—stop.

Since he had given up his night to stay with her and watch over Adam—in essence being the *only* one who stayed up with Adam after a point—Cassidy felt that she owed Will an update on Adam's condition.

It was, she argued with herself, the decent thing to do.

She was still telling herself that when she pulled up in front of his ranch house, parked her truck and got out. Crossing to the front door, Cassidy's nerve failed her just about the time she raised her hand to knock.

She stood there for a moment, her hand raised but

not making contact while she carried on an internal argument with herself.

Will could be out of the house, working on the range. He could be mending fences, training horses or any one of a dozen other things that would've necessitated his leaving the ranch house.

Instead of standing here, debating, Cassidy upbraided herself, she needed to get back to Adam and her responsibilities. She could leave Laredo a message on his phone since she felt she owed him an update.

Engrossed, she didn't hear the footsteps behind her. Not until Will was there, less than a foot away. She was just about to drop her hand to her side.

"Posing for a statue?" Will asked.

This time, she did shriek. Shrieked and swung around, her hand fisted and ready to make contact. Will barely jumped back in time.

"Hey, watch that, Champ," he chided, grabbing her wrist. "You nearly knocked me out."

Cassidy yanked her hand free. She wasn't swinging that hard. "Only if I had some kind of a weapon in my hand when I made contact," she told him sarcastically. "Or have you suddenly developed a glass jaw?"

"Nope, my jaw is hard as ever." His eyes swept over her. "And since you don't have a weapon in your hand, can I assume that you came by for a friendly chat?" he asked, opening his door. "Or did you change your mind about that loan you brought over the other day?"

"The answer's no to both," she informed him. "I just thought, after what you did last night, spending it watching Adam and all, I owed it to you to give you an update on his condition."

"Why don't you come inside?" he urged, pushing the door open even farther when she made no effort to follow him in. "The horses like to gossip. Before you know it, they'll be labeling us a couple, and everyone will be forced to believe it."

"Not if they had any sense," she informed him crisply. But after a moment, she gave in and walked into the house.

"Ah, well, there you have the problem in a nutshell." When she looked at him, puzzled, he went on to explain, "Having sense doesn't factor into it for most people." Taking off his jacket, Will tossed it onto his sofa. Then, turning back to look at Cassidy, he became serious. "So, how is he doing?"

He switched topics so quickly, she had to pause for a moment so her brain could catch up and make sense of his last question. She realized that the "he" Will was asking her about was Adam.

Of course it's Adam. Who else would it be? You just said you came here to give him an update on the boy.

What was it about Will lately that turned her into a simpleton, unable to rub two thoughts together?

"He's doing great," she told him, enthusiasm entering her voice. "His fever's completely gone and he's hungry." But Will probably already knew the latter since he'd fed Adam while she'd been asleep, she reminded herself. Cassidy pushed on, determined to tell him what she'd come to tell him and then leave. Fast. "It's like seeing a tiny miracle."

"That's what he is, all right," Will agreed, perching on the sofa's arm, "a tiny miracle."

She needed to go, Cassidy told herself. She was suddenly feeling awkward and definitely out of her element. Even so, she needed to know the answer to the main question that kept cropping up in her head.

"Why did you do it?"

Will glared at her. "'It'?" he repeated. "You're going to have to get a little more specific than that."

"Why did you stay with me at the clinic last night? You didn't have to. For that matter, why didn't you wake me up when Adam needed changing and when he had to be fed?" Until last night, she would have bet any amount of money that Will would have left those things up to her, not taken them upon himself to do—and certainly not without immediately taking credit for them.

Will pretended to be confused by her phrasing. "So are you asking me why I did something, or why I didn't do something?"

"Both," she retorted. And then she sighed, reining in her temper. She shouldn't have snapped at him. It was just that being around him like this unsettled her. "Why does everything have to be so difficult with you?"

Will grinned in response. "It's more memorable that way." He saw another hint of impatience crease her brow. It was a look he was intimately familiar with. For once, he didn't want to bait her. In the interest of a truce, he decided he might as well answer her questions without drawing out the process.

He did have things he needed to get to, Will reminded himself. The first of which was to put some distance between Cassidy and himself. The reason for that was a very basic one. He found himself entertaining some very strong thoughts, not to mention urges, regarding the two of them. If he didn't get some space between them—and soon—he was going to act on those urges.

He didn't relish the idea of rejection.

"But to answer your questions, I stayed with you last night because I felt you needed company. The night has a way of magnifying a person's fears, and I didn't want you up all night, worrying about Adam when he was going to be all right."

"And you knew that for a fact," she said sarcastically. The sarcasm was a defense mechanism. She needed a barrier between them, because she was having decidedly unsettling thoughts about him and she needed something to make her stay away. Something to make him *keep* her away.

Will ignored her tone. "Pretty much," he answered. "As for why I didn't wake you when Adam needed changing, well, that was beeause just before you fell asleep, you looked almost too exhausted to breathe. I thought I'd let you get some rest. Besides, I'm perfectly capable of changing a baby's diaper."

"Because of all your vast experience in changing diapers," she said, falling back on sarcasm again. If she didn't, she was in danger of just melting right in front of him. There was this look on his face that she was having trouble resisting.

"Not vast," he allowed, then added, "but I've had some."

"When?" Cassidy challenged. "When would you have possibly gotten experience changing diapers?"

He debated not saying anything, then decided he had nothing to lose. Besides, it was all in the past. And if it gave her ammunition to rag on him, well, so be it. "During those years I was away."

She was about to discount his statement when it suddenly hit her. Her eyes widened as she stared at Will. "You got married," she said. There was no joy in her voice, no celebratory tone for a friend. If anything, there was a note of crushing disappointment in her voice.

The simplest thing would have been to say yes—but it wasn't true. And he didn't lie.

"No."

Cassidy didn't think that she could feel so relieved over nothing—but she did.

"Then just how would you have gotten that experience with diaper changing?"

He smiled. Cassidy had overlooked a very uncomplicated answer to her question. "I briefly dated a woman with a baby, but I can't say I've had much experience."

He had always attracted women, all the way back to the fifth grade. But she couldn't picture him "dating" so much as just spending time and availing himself of the fruits that were being offered to him. Getting involved with a woman who had a baby was an entirely different scenario, and she was having trouble picturing him in it.

"You?"

"Yes, me." He shrugged, as if the whole thing was of less than no importance to him. "But then I came to my senses. I realized that she reminded me too much of you, so it was never going to work."

"She reminded you of me?" Cassidy questioned, stunned. "Is that why you dated her?"

"No, that's why I stopped," he said simply.

She felt dismissed, diminished. "I came to tell you about Adam because I felt like I owed it to you, but I must have been crazy. To willingly leave myself wide open like this so that you could parade your pathetic wit at my expense—"

"I dated her because she did make me think of you," he admitted to the back of her head.

Cassidy knew she was going to regret this, but she forced herself to turn to face him. "What did you say?"

The woman annoyed the hell out of him—and he wanted her so badly that he ached. What the hell was wrong with him?

"You heard me. She reminded me of you." And then he tried to put it in the proper perspective. "I guess I was kind of homesick after all, and being around some-one who looked like you was the closest I could get to home."

But Cassidy wasn't about to let this go. Not yet. "Then why did you break up with her?"

She had no idea how, but she could feel his eyes pulling her in and yet holding her in place at the same time.

Cassidy realized that she had to remind herself to breathe.

"Because she wasn't you."

Chapter Sixteen

Because they were so unexpected—the complete opposite of what she would have thought he'd say—it took a
couple of seconds for Will's words to sink in.

And another second before she could actually answer him. Her mouth felt dry as she told him, "I would
have thought, from your point of view, that would have
been a good thing."

Will slowly nodded, his dark blond hair falling into
his eyes.

"It should have been." His eyes held hers as he added,
"But it wasn't."

What had happened to all the space that had been between them, she couldn't help wondering. When she'd
turned, there'd been at least several strides between
where he was standing and where she'd stopped. But
somehow, in the last few seconds, they seemed to have
just vanished.

She didn't remember walking toward him. When
had he walked toward her? And why wasn't she turning and leaving now that he'd answered her question?

She wasn't leaving, she realized, because he *had* answered her question.

That and because she suddenly really, really wanted him to kiss her the way he had that one time, when he'd kissed her so deeply she became seriously in danger of forgetting how to ever walk again.

But as much as she found herself yearning for that kiss, she knew that if he didn't make the first move, she couldn't very well just throw herself at him. If she did, she'd never live it down because Laredo would never *let* her.

This was crazy.

She couldn't just go on standing there like some deer that had been caught in the proverbial headlights. She needed to leave.

Now.

"Well, I'd better be going," she heard herself saying, "since I did what I'd set out to do."

His presence seemed to be almost looming over her, making the rest of the area shrink away. "What's that? Drive me crazy?"

That would require a very short drive, she thought, biting her tongue.

"I came because I was trying to be nice," Cassidy reminded him.

"By driving me crazy," Will repeated, because that was exactly what she was doing, just by standing there—driving him crazy.

Driving him crazy because he wanted to touch her, to kiss her. To make love with her so badly he could scarcely breathe.

"Correct me if I'm wrong, but for once, we're not knee-deep in an argument."

Again, Laredo seemed to have come that much closer to her. He was so close now that if she took a deep breath, her chest was going to bump up against the lower part of his.

"Kind of leaves a void, doesn't it?" he asked her, commenting on her assessment.

"I don't notice a void," she told him defensively. Cassidy turned her face up to his so he could hear her better. Her voice cracked for some reason, as if she couldn't get in enough air to get her voice to carry the short distance between her mouth and his ears.

She struggled to keep from squirming.

"I do," he told her. "The void starts right about here," he went on, touching his chest and moving downward until he reached his lower abdomen. "And ends up here, cutting clear down to the bone."

"Maybe you should see someone about that," she suggested, the words all but falling from her lips in slow motion.

"I just might do that," he responded.

The next moment, there were no more words, no more nebulous speculations that went around in dizzying circles. Because the next moment, Will had finally given in to himself and lowered his mouth to hers, putting an end to the conversation and creating a whole new set of parameters for both of them.

She knew, *really* knew, that she should put a stop to what was happening. Right now. But "right now" seemed to perversely be slipping further and further away from her grasp. Further and further away from what she had, until she'd crossed this line, perceived to be reality.

Her reality.

Suddenly, she wasn't sure about anything, especially about the way she *thought* she felt about Will Laredo. Because if he was the man she loved to hate, why was every part of her lighting up like that huge Christmas tree that Miss Joan had the town decorate every year in the town square?

Light up like it? Hell, she mocked herself, she could easily out-glow it any day of the week and twice on Sundays.

She had dated a lot of cowboys in her time—thought at least three of them were "the one" in their own time. But she had never, ever felt about any of them the way she found herself feeling about Will Laredo. Like she wanted to seal herself to him forever.

Wouldn't Laredo get a laugh out of that if he knew, she thought, trying to work herself up and get angry. Angry enough to pull back and put a stop to this before it was too late.

But it was *already* too late because she didn't want to pull back, didn't want to put a stop to it. What she wanted, Cassidy realized—Lord help her—was to make love with him. Make love with Laredo the way no woman had ever made love with a man before. She was prepared to go down in flames and be reduced to a pile of ashes, as long as those ashes were mingled with *his*.

None of this was making any sense to her.

Maybe she had died plunging into the river after that

baby and this was all some wild, afterlife fantasy that had ensnared her.

She didn't know.

Didn't care.

All she cared about was finding a way to scratch this overwhelming itch she was feeling. An itch Will had created and that only he seemed to have the power to scratch for her.

HAD HE LOST his mind? This was *Cassidy* he was all but wrapped around like some giant piece of cellophane. Cassidy. His best friend's sister, for heaven's sake. The woman who would have sooner argued with him than breathe—and always did.

He was supposed to be doing everything in his power to avoid her, not trying to absorb her into his system as if she was every bit as vital to him for his survival as the very air.

He had to put a *stop* to this.

And yet, every second that he was kissing Cassidy only had him wanting to kiss her that much more. Who would have ever guessed that her lips tasted this good, this tempting, this life-affirming?

Certainly not him.

And yet here he was, kissing her. Wanting her. Wanting more.

The little voice in his head that was so heavily grounded in common sense told him to stop, to make her leave. And if she wouldn't, then he was the one who needed to leave. Right this second.

Hell, he needed to run as if the town's villagers were all coming after him with pitchforks and torches.

But he didn't run, he didn't stop.

He couldn't.

Not when he was on fire this way.

Hell, he could barely remember his own name, much less how to walk away. He certainly couldn't *run*.

Will felt his head spinning so badly, he was certain that he'd fall on the floor if he made a move away from her.

So instead, he made a move *on* her.

With his mouth still sealed to hers, he began to undress Cassidy. To open buttons, tug out shirttails, unnotch the belt on her jeans. He wanted her completely to himself, the way she'd been created.

Completely and utterly nude.

CASSIDY'S HEART WAS racing so hard, she thought it would burst right out of her chest. Not only was Laredo making the entire world around them shrink to the head of a pin and then just disappear, he was making her body temperature climb to dangerous heights in anticipation of each and every move.

She urgently pulled at Will's clothing, stripping him of his shirt, trying to tug off his jeans until she realized that she'd overlooked one important thing. Or rather, two.

"Your boots, take off your boots," she half begged, half ordered.

And when Will didn't seem to understand what she

was saying, or to execute her order fast enough, Cassidy did it herself.

Half nude, she began pulling at his boots, frustrated and eager at the same time.

He thought he'd never seen anything more beautiful in his life.

The moment his boots were off, Will maneuvered out of his jeans.

And then there were no more barriers between them. They were free to do whatever they wanted to.

But rather than take her there and then, the way she'd anticipated that he would, Will surprised her by continuing to up the ante. He did things to her that primed her body and made her anticipation all the greater.

Will made love to every single part of her before he culminated in making love to the whole of her the way she'd been waiting for him to do.

Before that final moment came, he'd made all of her quiver, all of her feel the small, hard surges of climaxes flowering one after the other until she was quite certain that her entire body was spent and there was nothing more left within her to feel anything else.

But she was wrong.

Because after the caresses, after the long, moist kisses along the length of her body that had her twisting and turning beneath his mouth in absolute sweet, sweeping agony and bliss, Cassidy discovered that there was one last, pulsating reserve she had left to offer up to Will.

With his fingers entwined and locked with hers, he slid his body over Cassidy's and into position. With his eyes watching hers, he entered her and took what had already become his from the moment this dance between them had begun.

His hips against hers, he began to move, urging her to follow until she started to keep up with him.

In sync, they moved faster and faster in anticipation of that one last glorious moment when their union would be finalized in a wondrous shower involving stars, fireworks and blazing sensations. A moment when free-floating was the norm, not the exception.

And when it happened, when it finally captured them both, Will held on to her even more tightly than he had before, as if the thought of letting go meant permanently letting go of her.

Time froze, then slowly moved forward again, bringing back reality as it reluctantly let go of euphoria.

HIS HEART WOULDN'T stop hammering, as if it was meant to break free of its earthly shell and then meld with the stars overhead. For a few minutes, Will thought that it was going to, leaving him behind in the process—a broken vessel in its wake.

It still took a while for his heart to finally stop pounding. It took longer than that for him to catch his breath.

What the hell had they just done?

Will felt her stiffening beside him, felt the exact second when reality returned to her like a tsunami immediately after an earthquake.

Will caught himself thinking that that was almost appropriate, considering that, at least for him, the earth had definitely moved the way it never had before.

For a fraction of a moment, because it was against his nature to restrain someone who wanted to leave, Will thought of letting her bolt. Of letting Cassidy leave—if that was what she really wanted—without him saying a single word to stop her. He didn't want to prolong whatever she was feeling right at this second that was making her want to flee.

But another part of him, the new, improved part of him that had just been made to see the light, didn't want Cassidy fleeing. He didn't want her acting as if this was all one giant mistake that could somehow be erased with enough denial—especially if it was *mutual* denial.

Most of all, he didn't want to deny what had just happened.

Because to him, what had just happened bordered on a miracle.

And no good ever came of denying a miracle, especially when that miracle had just unaccountably landed right smack in their laps.

The way this one had.

So he closed his arms around Cassidy rather than letting her bolt off the sofa. And when she tried to wiggle free of his grip, he only held on to her that much more tightly.

"Let me go!" she cried, angry at herself for what she'd allowed to happen and angry at him for fueling the flames of a fire that just refused to go out.

He made no move to do anything of the kind. "Not yet. Not until you calm down," he told her.

"Okay. I'm calm," she declared between gritted teeth. "Now let me go!"

"Saying it isn't going to make it so," he told her in a voice she found maddeningly poised and self-contained.

His calm tone just made her angrier. "You can't hold me prisoner like this!"

"Maybe not," he said agreeably. "But I can dream. And for the record, I'm not holding you prisoner, I'm just holding you."

She would have thought that he, of all men, would have wanted to put distance between himself and a woman once the act of lovemaking was over. Will Laredo was the original carefree bachelor.

Just what was he up to?

"Why?" she challenged.

"Because you're soft and, heaven help me, I like holding you. And, in case it escaped your notice, something really nice just happened here. Now, whether you want to admit it or not, it *did* happen, and I suspect that a part of you really enjoyed it despite your protests. I know that more than a part of me did. Actually, I'd say that *all* of me did."

She was not about to admit to anything of the kind. The only thing she would admit was that she was agitated about what had just happened. Agitated because all of her life she'd told herself that she couldn't bide Will Laredo, and now to discover otherwise—to discover the exact opposite—well, it was too much for her to absorb all at once. And definitely too much for her to acknowledge.

Cassidy needed time to come to grips with this. Time and space, and she needed it *now*.

"I've got to go," she insisted. "I left Adam with Connor."

"Wise choice," he told her approvingly, a fact that only got her that much more agitated. "Connor's levelheaded."

She was disoriented and disappointed with herself. Will's words had her instantly jumping to a conclusion. "And I'm not, is that what you're trying to say?"

This was going to take patience, possibly more patience than he had. But he would give it his best shot.

"No, what I'm trying to say is don't run. Because no matter how fast you try to go, that feeling you're trying to outrun is going to catch up to you."

"Maybe," she said, pulling away from him and finally getting up. "But I've still got to try."

Clutching her clothes to her like a makeshift shield, Cassidy backed out of the room and then hurried away to get dressed.

She needed to make good her escape before he broke through her resolve—again.

Chapter Seventeen

Christmas was just a few days away, and Cassidy purposely made herself busier than ever. Christmas had always been her favorite time of year, and it didn't have anything to do with the anticipation of gifts.

For her, it had never really been about gifts—at least not the store-bought kind. The gift of family and love was what was and had always been of major importance for Cassidy. Everything else came second, but she still immersed herself in it. Currently she had her internship at the firm and her online classes to juggle, not to mention that she was taking care of the baby and still finding time to decorate the house for Christmas, something that had always been, without a doubt, her very favorite "chore."

While she kept herself busy with all of this, Cassidy was doing her damnedest not to dwell on what had gone down between Will and her—or even think about it. But her resolve seemed to be made out of vapor, and trying *not* to think about having made love with Laredo just caused her to dwell on it that much more in her unguarded moments. Moments that, for some reason, seemed to be cropping up more and more as the days went by.

The only thing she was grateful for was that neither Connor nor Cole said anything about what had become the elephant in the room.

But finally Connor gave up on trying to stay out of Cassidy's business. So he confronted her in the kitchen late one afternoon.

It must have been obvious that she just wanted to avoid any sort of conversation with him about anything other than Adam or the approaching holiday.

When she tried to get around him, he blocked her exit from the kitchen and bluntly asked, "Okay, what's up with you and Will?"

Cassidy pretended to look at him blankly, as if his changing the subject to Will hadn't caused her to abruptly shut down and try to leave the room.

"Nothing's up with us," she replied crisply. "I find him the same irritating creature I always have."

"No," Connor contradicted her, matching her every move so that she couldn't leave the room, "you're going out of your way to avoid him when he comes by."

Cassidy blew out an annoyed breath. "*Because* I find him the same irritating creature I always have."

"No, that's a lot of bull. Something's changed," Connor insisted. "It has ever since you came home last week after running your 'errands' the day after Adam was in the clinic."

Cassidy scowled. She was not about to have a heart-to-heart with her big brother. Those days had long passed. She was a grown woman and was entitled to live her life without interference. Nowhere did it say she had to open up about what she was feeling.

"You're letting your imagination run away with you," she said dismissively.

There was a knowing look in Connor's eyes as he said, "It wasn't my imagination that noticed the buttons on your blouse were misaligned that day."

Cassidy opened her mouth and then closed it again, momentarily at a loss as to how to respond. Her brother had definitely caught her off guard.

Connor just continued, "I might not have as much schooling as you do, but I'm not just a hayseed cowboy, Cassidy. I do notice things—and you were gone a long time that day. Are you going to tell me that you were running errands all that time?"

That was exactly what she wanted to tell him, but the words seemed to be sticking in her throat. She didn't make it a habit of lying to Connor, but neither did she want to be drawn out on the carpet and treated like a child.

She looked at him defiantly. "Would you believe me if I did?"

"If you swore that it was the truth, I'd have to." He looked into her eyes, wanting to believe that the relationship they'd always had of mutual respect was still alive and well. "Are you?"

She bit the bottom of her lip. She really wanted to swear to him that it was the truth. Because it would put an end to Connor's speculations about her and Laredo, which were definitely coming too close to the truth for comfort.

But she had never once lied to Connor, and she couldn't allow her desire to block that whole day out of her life to cause her to lie to Connor now.

"No," she finally said, defiance in her tone.

He could always read her, although at times it took some effort. "My guess is that you're avoiding Will because it went too well and that scares you."

Cassidy tossed her head. "Nothing scares me," she informed him. "Now I've got a test to study for—" Adam's cries broke through the conversation. "And a baby to change, and I've still got a few gifts to wrap. None of which are going to take care of themselves, so can we table this conversation about a man who makes my blood pressure rise for now?"

"We're going to have to have it sooner or later," he pointed out.

Circumventing Connor, Cassidy crossed into the living room and picked up Adam from the playpen. She began patting his back automatically in soothing concentric circles.

"Later. I vote for later." As she started to leave for her bedroom to change the baby, there was a knock on the front door. She glanced over her shoulder at Connor. The latter was already heading toward the door. "You expecting anyone?" she asked him, a hint of wariness entering her voice.

Cody and Cole were both at work. Besides, neither one of them would knock. Connor shook his head. "Nobody I can think of."

When he opened the door, he found Will standing there.

"You're right," Cassidy commented as she turned away and began to walk up the stairs. "It's nobody."

But Will wasn't about to get drawn into a sarcastic verbal battle. He addressed her back, his voice somewhat strained and formal. "Cassidy, you might want to wait up. This concerns you, too."

But Cassidy just kept on going up the stairs. "There's nothing that you can say that concerns me, Laredo," she retorted.

He didn't bother arguing with her. He just told her the headline. "They found Adam's mother."

Cassidy's arms tightened around Adam as she froze. She put one hand on the banister to steady herself before turning. Her eyes on Will, she came back down. Her mind was going everywhere at once, trying to think, to anticipate what came next.

"Who found her?" she asked him in a stilted voice.

Will came closer to the staircase. "The sheriff and Joe, acting on an anonymous call from someone on the reservation."

Her insides were quivering as Cassidy desperately tried to steel herself. She wasn't succeeding very well.

She didn't remember coming back down the stairs. All she was aware of was that her legs felt rubbery. Her voice sounded hollow to her own ears as she asked, "When will she be coming for the baby?"

"She won't be," Will told her quietly. Before Cassidy could ask him anything else, he added, "They found her in her car. It must have washed up at the edge of the reservation a month ago. There was water in her lungs. She drowned in that flash flood."

"How do they know she was Adam's mother?" Connor asked.

Will's eyes shifted over to his friend. "Joe said they found some baby things in the car, and she had this locket around her neck. There was a picture of the baby pasted inside it."

All three of them were now standing in a small circle. The only one oblivious to the gravity of the conversation was its subject. Adam.

Connor glanced at the boy. "No offense to Adam, but a lot of babies at his age look the same if you shrink their picture down to locket size," he said.

"Which was why Joe stayed on the reservation, following up," Will told them. "Joe figured that since he originally came from there, if he kept at it long enough, someone would talk to him and tell him what happened."

"And?" Cassidy asked, prodding him.

"And he found the girl's aunt who, with enough prodding told Joe the whole story. Seems Adam's mother, Miriam Morning Star, was taking Adam and leaving the reservation the morning the flash flood hit. She was going to go look for Adam's father, a college kid who, along with some other students, had volunteered to work on the reservation a year ago."

Connor, listening, nodded. "I remember. There were ten of them as I recall."

Will nodded. "Miriam and the volunteer had a brief relationship, and then he went back to school. A few letters were exchanged, and then he stopped writing— around the time she told him she was pregnant. Miriam's aunt said that the girl got it into her head that once the baby's father saw Adam—who, by the way, she called Joshua—they'd be a family. Except that she never got too far off the reservation. From the looks of it, the car was engulfed by the floodwater. Miriam lost control."

"And they only found the car now?" Cassidy questioned incredulously.

"The car was partially hidden by debris. Hey, there was a lot of land to cover for three deputies," he reminded Cassidy, "and don't forget, her aunt thought she'd left the reservation. When the truth dawned on her, she wasn't overly eager to talk about a niece who had shamed her ancestors and turned her back on her heritage by giving herself to an 'outsider.'"

"Does the aunt want to take Adam?" Cassidy asked in a wary voice. She was trying to figure out what sort of recourse she had open to her. He might represent a lot of work, but she had gotten very attached to Adam in the last month.

Will shook his head. "She wants him to go to a stable home. She told Joe to do as he sees fit."

"Nobody else in the family?" Connor asked, remembering his own circumstances when he'd taken over as his siblings' guardian. There'd been no other family members.

"Not from anything that Joe heard," Will answered. "And he asked around."

At least that threat was gone, Cassidy thought, suddenly coming to.

"Well, unclaimed or not, Adam still needs his diaper changed. I'll be right back," she said.

"I'll be here," Will called after her.

"That's what I'm afraid of," Cassidy murmured, although loud enough for Will to overhear.

SHE TOOK HER time changing the baby, letting the full import of the information that Will had just finished telling them sink in.

"Well, Adam, it looks like you really are an orphan after all. What do you think we should do about that?" she asked.

The baby made a gurgling noise as if in response, and she laughed softly as she finished changing him.

"Oh, you do, do you?" she said as if the baby had said something intelligible. "Well, I'm going to have to think about that, but I've got a feeling that I might not have all that much time to think. Sometimes things actually do move fast around here." She sighed. "Usually when you don't want them to. Word might get back to social services up in the county." She picked Adam up, thinking how good he felt in her arms. "The truth of it is, I've gotten very used to having you hanging around, even if I don't sleep much anymore.

"Besides, if you're not around, what'll I do with those Christmas presents I bought for you?" Adam made more unintelligible noises, to which she nodded and said, "My thoughts exactly."

When she brought Adam downstairs again, she was all set to announce that she was going to adopt Adam. She clung to the fact that she had been caring for him all this time and that it would act in her favor.

"I get it," Will said the moment she started coming

down. Apparently he'd been waiting at the foot of the stairs since she'd gone up.

She had no idea what Laredo was referring to. "Get what?"

"I get it if you don't want to adopt Adam."

"I don't want to adopt Adam?" she echoed, stunned. Just where had he gotten that idea? She'd never said anything of the kind. To be fair, she had never said anything one way or the other about Adam's future.

"Because if you don't want to," Will continued, "then I'll adopt him."

"You?" Cassidy said in disbelief, her tone mocking the very idea.

Connor stepped in and deftly took Adam from her. Her hands free, she fisted them on her hips as she faced Will.

Will felt his back going up. "Yes, what's wrong with that?"

Was he kidding? "Because, in case you forgot that you've always had this love 'em and leave 'em reputation, everyone else around here remembers and that, my friend," she informed him, "is why you wouldn't have a snowball's chance in hell of adopting this baby."

Rather than get annoyed, Will actually smiled at her dismissal. "I've changed—"

To which she responded, "Ha!"

"And I can make further changes," Will continued as if he was already arguing his case before a family court judge. "I can make all the changes necessary in order to be regarded as a good father for the baby."

"Oh?" This was going to be good, Cassidy thought. "And what changes can you possibly make?"

Will dropped the ultimate bombshell. "I can get married."

For a second, Cassidy's jaw dropped, but she came around the next moment. "What woman in her right mind would have you?"

"Well, I guess that rules you out because you've never been in your right mind."

Angry, Cassidy glared at him. How could she have thought that there was something between them? She must have been delirious when she'd made love with this man. Well, she was definitely over him now and thinking straight again.

"I'll have you know that I am very much in my right mind!" she informed him.

"Fine!" he shouted. "Then will you marry me?"

Connor was about to break up the argument when he heard Will's unorthodox proposal and pulled back.

Cassidy was still running on fury. Fury that came to an abrupt halt in the middle of her response. "What the hell are you yelling at me for— Wait, what?" She stared at Will. "Did you just ask me to marry you?" she demanded, stunned close to speechlessness.

She expected Will to laugh at her and tell her that it was all a joke.

But he didn't laugh, didn't say it was a joke.

Instead, what Will did say was "Yes."

She refused to believe he was serious. There was a punch line here somewhere. "You actually want to marry me?" she asked.

The corners of his mouth curved, all but undoing her entirely. "Amazingly enough, yes, I do."

"You want to marry *me*?" she asked again, unable to believe he wasn't somehow setting her up for a fall.

"Pay attention, Adam," Connor said to the baby he was holding. "Your future dad's well-intentioned but kind of slow-witted at times." He turned toward Will. "She's waiting for you to say the words, Will, so say them. Ask her to marry you," he prompted.

Will felt as if he was standing in the middle of someone else's dream—until he realized that it was his dream, that maybe it had *always* been his dream and that only the fear of rejection had put him in denial all these years.

Taking a deep breath, Will plunged in. "Cassidy McCullough, will you marry me?"

Cassidy still held back. "Are you sure that you're not going to shout 'April Fool's' or something like that if I say yes?"

"It's December 21. That's a long ways away from April Fool's," he told her.

"Take a leap of faith, Cassidy," Connor urged. "And know that I've got your back. If this turns out to be an elaborate hoax, I'll skin him alive for you. Now answer the man," he ordered.

She closed her eyes and took a breath, then opened her eyes again. Will was still there, waiting. She said, "Yes!"

Rather than any proclamations of an elaborate joke being in play, Will echoed "Yes!" as well, then threw his arms around her. Lifting Cassidy off the ground, he kissed her. Long and hard and with all his heart.

Connor waited a moment, then, when it looked like a moment wasn't going to be nearly long enough for his sister and his best friend, he politely turned away from them.

"C'mon, Adam, let's give them some privacy. This looks like it's going to take a while. Grown-ups are funny like that. But the bottom line is that you've got your mom and dad, and that's all that really counts."

Epilogue

It was perfect.

Absolutely perfect.

Cassidy scanned the area and smiled to herself in tired satisfaction.

The tree was up and finally decorated. That had been touch and go for a while. All the gifts that she was in charge of were wrapped and under the tree—finished just by the skin of her teeth, she thought with a grin, if teeth had skin. The spiral ham was in the oven, its aroma competing with the heady scent of pine. Even the table was set.

Everything was ready, including her, for the celebratory dinner that had become a tradition: Christmas Eve dinner.

They had come a long way, Cassidy couldn't help thinking, from that first Christmas she and her brothers had spent the year their father had died. Back then Connor barely had enough money for them to scrape by. Christmas Eve dinner that year was in Miss Joan's house—she had insisted on it.

Cassidy could remember being surprised that Miss

Joan actually *had* a house. She had just assumed that the woman lived in the diner. To her thirteen-year-old mind, it had seemed that way.

The jingling noise drew her attention toward the playpen.

Adam was all dressed up and entertaining himself with the silver bells on his shoelaces. Apparently the ringing sound reduced him to giggles.

Cassidy couldn't remember hearing a more heart-warming sound than Adam's laughter.

A delayed chill filled the room, and Cassidy realized that Connor had opened the door. Cody, Devon and their daughter, Layla, had come in.

"What is that wonderful smell?" Devon asked as she shrugged out of her coat while Cody held their daughter in his arms.

"That," Connor informed her, "is a genuine Christmas miracle. Cassidy made dinner and nothing's burned."

"Evening's still young," Cody responded with a laugh.

"Just for that," Cassidy said, looking at her brother as she came forward to greet his family, "you don't get to eat anything."

"I'll have to reserve judgment on whether that's a good thing or a bad thing," Cody told her, then ducked as Cassidy took a swing at his arm.

"Don't listen to him," Devon told her sister-in-law. "When's dinner? We're starved."

"We can start as soon as everyone's here," Connor told her.

"Well, I'm here," Cole declared, overhearing his older brother as he came down the stairs.

Cody looked at Connor. "That's everybody, right?"

"Not quite," Connor told him.

"I thought you said this was strictly a family dinner," Cody reminded his brother, looking toward Cassidy for an answer. "Who else is coming?"

There was a knock on the door just then. "I think that's your answer," Connor told him. He was about to go open the door, but Cassidy managed to get ahead of him. With a smile, Connor dropped back.

Cole and Cody exchanged glances, but neither had an answer for the other. Connor caught the look. "You'll see," he promised his brothers, a rather satisfied smile playing on his lips.

The next moment he saw that both of his brothers appeared completely stunned when Will walked in across the threshold. They grew more so when they saw Will kiss their sister.

Granted it was a quick kiss, but they both expected Cassidy to read their friend the riot act just before she punched him in the gut—but none of that happened.

"What's wrong with Cassidy?" Cole asked. The question was echoed by Cody.

"Not a thing, boys," Connor answered. "Not a thing." He beckoned his family into the living room.

"Why's your camera set up?" Cody asked. The old-fashioned camera—a gift from Miss Joan—had recorded all their milestones over the years. Connor saw to that. But they hadn't seen the camera out and mounted on its tripod since Cody and Devon's wedding.

"I thought it might be nice to get a family picture of all of us together," Connor answered.

Cody slanted a glance toward his sister, expecting some sort of a tirade, or at the very least a dismissal of Connor's suggestion. While he and his brothers all thought of Will as family, Cassidy had made it clear that she thought of Will as the lowest form of lowlife.

"Aren't you going to say anything?" Cody asked his sister, mystified.

"Yes," she replied.

"Finally," Cody whispered to his wife.

"I think that we should take the picture before we have dinner. That way, nobody has to worry about hiding a gravy stain or some other food that's on your clothes—that's not to say that I don't appreciate you eating with gusto, because I do."

"Okay," Cole cried. "What's going on here? I feel like I've just fallen into some alternate universe or whatever they called it in those science-fiction movies Dad used to like to fall asleep to on late-night TV."

"Well," Will began, "I was going to wait until everyone started opening their gifts, but maybe I should do this now."

"Do *what* now?" Cole asked impatiently.

"You know what's going on?" he asked Cody only to have Cody shake his head.

"Do you?" Cole turned toward Connor.

To his surprise, Connor nodded.

Before Cole could quiz his older brother for an expla-nation, he heard Will say, "This was my grandmother's, and she left it to me, saying that if I ever found that one special woman who I wanted to spend the rest of my life with, I should give it to her." He opened his hand then and held it up to Cassidy.

A small, square-cut diamond ring was in the center of his palm, sparkling as it caught some of the lights coming from the Christmas tree.

"So I'm giving it to you, Cassidy—if you'll have it—and me."

Cassidy could barely suppress the grin that was fight-ing to take over her entire face. "Well, since you twisted my arm, I guess I can't say no and embarrass you in front of your friends."

"Never stopped you before," Cole quipped, still rather confused.

"Shut up, Cole," Cody chided, finally seeing the light. "You're spoiling the moment."

"You're wrong," Cassidy told him as she held out her hand toward Will and he slipped the ring on the third finger of her left hand. "Nothing can spoil this moment."

Especially, she thought, *since the ring fit.*

Several moments later, her eyes shining, she took her place beside Will who was holding their soon-to-be-adopted son. Her brothers, sister-in-law and niece flanked them on either side.

Connor quickly set the timer on the camera, then

darted back into place, instructing them to all say "Happiness!"

It was a good word, Cassidy thought, leaning into Will, because she couldn't remember ever feeling happier than she did right at this moment.

* * * * *

Don't miss Marie Ferrarella's next book,
TWICE A HERO, ALWAYS HER MAN,
coming in January 2017 from
Mills & Boon Cherish.

MILLS & BOON®

Cherish™

EXPERIENCE THE ULTIMATE RUSH OF FALLING IN LOVE

A sneak peek at next month's titles...

In stores from 15th December 2016:

- **Slow Dance with the Best Man** – Sophie Pembroke
  and **A Fortune in Waiting** – Michelle Major
- **Her New Year Baby Secret** – Jessica Gilmore
  and **Twice a Hero, Always Her Man** – Marie Ferrarella

In stores from 29th December 2016:

- **The Prince's Convenient Proposal** – Barbara Hannay
  and **His Ballerina Bride** – Teri Wilson
- **The Tycoon's Reluctant Cinderella** – Therese
  Beharrie *and* **The Cowboy's Runaway Bride** –
  Nancy Robards Thompson

Just can't wait?
Buy our books online a month before they hit the shops!
www.millsandboon.co.uk

Also available as eBooks.

MILLS & BOON®

EXCLUSIVE EXTRACT

When Eloise Miller finds herself thrown into the role of
maid of honour at the wedding of the year, her plans to
stay away from the gorgeous best man are scuppered!

Read on for a sneak preview of
SLOW DANCE WITH THE BEST MAN
by Sophie Pembroke

Maid of honour for Melissa Sommers. How on earth
had this happened? And the worst part was—

'Sounds like we'll be spending even more time
together.' Noah's voice was warm, deep and far too close
to her ear.

Eloise sighed. That. That was the worst thing. Because
the maid of honour was *expected* to pair up with the
best man, and that would not make her resolution to stay
away from Noah Cross any easier at all.

She turned and found him standing directly behind
her, close enough that if she'd stepped back a centimetre
or two she'd have been in his arms. Suddenly she was
glad he'd alerted her to his presence with his words.

She shifted further away and tried to look like a
professional, instead of a teenager with a crush. Looking
up at him, she felt the strange heat flush over her skin
again at his gorgeousness. Then she focused, and realised
he was frowning.

'Apparently so,' she agreed. 'But I'm sure I'll be far
too busy with all the wedding arrangements—'

'Oh, I doubt it,' Noah interrupted, but he still didn't sound entirely happy about the idea, which surprised her. Perhaps she'd misread his flirting earlier. Maybe he really was like that with everyone and, now the reality of having to spend time with her had set in, he was less keen on the idea. 'Melissa has quite the packed schedule for the wedding party, you know. She's right—you're going to have to find someone to take over most of your job here.'

Eloise sighed. She *did* know. She'd helped Laurel plan it, after all.

And, now she thought about it, every last bit of the schedule involved the maid of honour and the best man being together.

Noah smiled, a hint of the charm he'd exhibited earlier showing through despite the frown, and Eloise's heart beat twice in one moment as she accepted the inevitable.

She was doomed.

She had the most ridiculous crush on a man who clearly found her a minor inconvenience.

And—even worse—the whole world was going to be watching, laughing at her pretending that she could live in this world of celebrities, mocking her for thinking she could ever be pretty enough, funny enough…just *enough* for Noah Cross.

Don't miss
SLOW DANCE WITH THE BEST MAN
by Sophie Pembroke

Available January 2017
www.millsandboon.co.uk

Give a 12 month subscription to a friend today!

Call Customer Services
0844 844 1358*

or visit
millsandboon.co.uk/subscriptions

MILLS & BOON®

Why shop at millsandboon.co.uk?

Each year, thousands of romance readers find their perfect read at millsandboon.co.uk. That's because we're passionate about bringing you the very best romantic fiction. Here are some of the advantages of shopping at www.millsandboon.co.uk:

* **Get new books first**—you'll be able to buy your favourite books one month before they hit the shops

* **Get exclusive discounts**—you'll also be able to buy our specially created monthly collections, with up to 50% off the RRP

* **Find your favourite authors**—latest news, interviews and new releases for all your favourite authors and series on our website, plus ideas for what to try next

* **Join in**—once you've bought your favourite books, don't forget to register with us to rate, review and join in the discussions

Visit **www.millsandboon.co.uk**
for all this and more today!